MW01264312

PRAISE FOR JOSEPH RANSOM

"I never cease to be amazed at Joseph's skills and abilities...He is determined to serve his Lord by serving others." *Ron Boutwell, Executive Director, Stained Glass Theatre*

"Joseph's dramatic portrayals and captivating writing style show a depth of spiritual insight that is truly refreshing...He skillfully blends light hearted humor with spiritual depth. As a playwright, dramatist, Bible teacher and author, Joseph has ministered to my heart." *Jennifer Rothschild, Author*

"...Dr. Ransom is a proven communicator. He very effectively gets his message to people because of the unique combination of motivation and inspiration experienced by his listeners....He is a gifted author, actor, preacher, speaker and teacher. I can recommend him without any reservations. Anyone who engages his services will be enthusiastic about the results." *Dr. Paul Collins, ACTS Ministry*

"On numerous occasions I have had the opportunity to observe Joseph's dramatic presentations. Each time, I feel as though I have been placed into a time machine and transported back to Biblical days...Having known Joseph for several years, I can attest not only to his talents and abilities, but also to the godly character he exhibits. He has a tremendous desire to serve God in all that he does..." *Terry Maughon, Executive Director, Doe River Gorge Camp*

<u>PRAISE FOR "THE HEALING CITY"</u>

"As I was going to bed last night I thought I would read a few pages of your book...I set it down about 2 o'clock or so having read it from cover to cover!...You have a best seller on your hands!" *Joe Walker, College Instructor*

"An excellent story which reveals the unique experience when Christianity and the life of the cowboy become one." *Purity Publications*

"In *The Healing City* Dr. Joseph reminds us that the cowboy spirit is alive and well. It is what is right in America. The characteristics of honesty, integrity and hard work are more than principles from the West- they are principles from the Word. If Jesus had been born in Montana, His stories may have been of the Good Cowboy instead of the Good Shepherd....Whatever He's called you to do- it's time to Cowboy up!" *John Hill, Evangelist, Christian Magician*

"...Captures the reader from the first page." *D.G., Professional Editor*

"...You have a conversational and easy going story telling style that readers will find quite enjoyable...A charming and engaging story." *Vicki, Professional Editor*

THE HEALING CITY

A Cowboy Christmas Story

BY

JOSEPH RANSOM

This book is loosely based on actual events. Characters and incidents have been fictionalized for dramatic purposes.

"The Healing City," by Joseph Ransom. ISBN 978-1-60264-024-5.

Published 2007 by Virtualbookworm.com Publishing Inc., P.O. Box 9949, College Station, TX 77842, US. ©2007, Joseph Ransom. All rights reserved. No part of this publication may be reproduced, stored in a retrieval system, or transmitted in any form or by any means, electronic, mechanical, recording or otherwise, without the prior written permission of Joseph Ransom.

Manufactured in the United States of America.

© 2007 Cover design by Kaye Ransom

Ronan, Montana

Dedication

With love and sincere appreciation, this story is dedicated to Ralph Irwin, who is more than just a model of a man. Ralph, you are an example of a man of God. Thank you for reminding me daily that even a Montana cowboy can use his dreams for the glory of God.

Special thanks to Shelly Young at Marketplace Printing in Ozark, MO for cover assistance, the Natural Resources Conservation Service, and Bryan and Sherri Caperton of Bear Creek Trail Rides.

TABLE OF CONTENTS

THE HEALING CITY

PROLOGUE

Comfortable. That was the word that always came to mind as he entered the room. It was his favorite room of the house. Always had been. The only room that was truly his. Over the years, his library had developed a personality of its own. It wasn't planned that way, it just happened. To a visitor it may have looked disorganized, with its piles of books that overflowed the bookshelves surrounding the fireplace but he knew where every book lived. There were few pictures on the walls; there wasn't room for such things with his shelves that extended floor to ceiling, wall to wall. In fact, the only evidence of a woman's touch at all was in the bay window with its cushioned seat and small table with two matching chairs. The table was where he and his wife of more than forty years began and ended each day with an open Bible and a cup of coffee. She had wanted to put heavy drapes over the window to keep out the cold Montana winter, but he would never allow it. After all, this was his private room and his private view. It was one of those mountain views that were spectacular no matter what time of day, no matter what season of the year. In the end he did, after much persuasion, allow her to hang a valance across the top of the window, and he even let her cushion the window seat with matching material. She had long ago stopped trying to persuade him that the room did not fit the rest of the house. For her, it was too rustic, even for a home in the Montana mountains. But this home, or at least this room, was his private domain and she enjoyed how much he loved it. Besides, when he needed to think something out, or as was more likely the case, when he needed to pray something out, this was where he found his answers. Even on the rare occasions when they had had a disagreement, she knew that he, with his Bible, would find solace and peace in this room. And wasn't that more important than having a room out of *Home and Garden* magazine?

He sighed deeply as he glanced at the softly lit Christmas tree in the corner, then *slowly ambled across the room, not even noticing that he winced slightly as he took off his leather work coat. He gently laid it over the back of his favorite overstuffed chair, the one nearest the crackling, glowing fireplace. The wince was partly due to age, but mostly due to being bucked off Old Thunder too many times. Thunder had been gone for years now, but every day he lived with the reminders of what it meant to be a Montana cowboy. Thunder, the name alone brought back memories. Or maybe it was the weather that brought back the memories of so long ago. He had lived through many blizzards over the years, but none were as severe as that other Christmas; the one that began without warning. The one that...*

His trip down memory lane was suddenly, and loudly, interrupted as little Katie, with her pigtails bobbing up and down, galloped into the room on her much loved, and well-worn, stick horse.

"Whoa, there, Thunder. Howdy, Grandpa." He smiled at five-year-old Katie as he remembered her insisting on naming her stick horse 'Thunder' after hearing his stories of 'Thunder, the meanest stallion in the west'.

"Howdy, Pardner", he drawled in his exaggerated voice, the voice he saved for five-year-old granddaughters with pigtails

and stick horses named 'Thunder'.

Katie held tightly to the reins, as if afraid that Thunder would indeed buck her off. "Grandma said to tell you it's time for grub."

"Then you had better go put Thunder in the stable. And remember to brush him real good first."

"Oh, Grandpa, you're silly."

"Tell Grandma I'll be right in."

Katie stopped at the door, almost afraid to mention what she was thinking. Afraid of what the answer would be. "Grandpa?"

"What is it, Pardner?"

Katie half-smiled. "Grandpa, is it time yet?"

His memories of a long-ago blizzard both chilled and warmed his heart.

"Time? Time for what?"

"Come on, Grandpa, you're teasing me. It's time for you to read the Cowboy Christmas story. Like you do every year."

His heart was warmed by knowing that his favorite story was also her favorite story. He would enjoy the moment as long as possible.

"Is it Christmas already? It can't be!"

"Stop teasing. See, there's the tree. And here's the book. Right on your table by the fireplace; where you always put it. Now don't skip anything."

He couldn't help but smile. "If I can find my glasses."

Katie looked very much like the grown up she pretended to be as she raised her finger and pointed accusingly at her favorite person in the whole wide world. "Grandpa, they're on your head, like they always are. Besides, you prob'ly have the story mem'rized by now."

"That's true, but there's nothing like reading favorite words on a page. But what about your Grandma? She said the grub's on the table."

"Come on, Grandpa, supper can wait. When you don't show up, you know she'll come looking for you here. Please!"

Grandpa laughed as only a grandpa can laugh as he sank his weary bones down deep into his favorite chair and took the well-worn book from her hands. The book that was almost as worn and loved as Katie's stick horse. It was as Katie said; he knew the words by heart, but he still glanced lovingly at the faded and dog-eared pages as his mind and heart slipped back in time, as easily as a cowhand slips into a familiar saddle. He didn't even notice, and Katie had no reason to remind him, that his glasses were still on top of his head.

His voice started as the voice of a storyteller, but soon became the voice of a much younger man as he once again traveled far away, not in miles but in time. Katie gently laid down her stick horse and occasionally thought to pet his soft mane as she sat at Grandpa's feet and once again heard her favorite story; the story that Grandpa had memorized, not just with his mind but with his heart. He tenderly wrapped Katie in his old leather work coat. Neither Katie nor Grandpa noticed or cared that the blizzard outside was bringing in cold air around the window as Grandpa read the opening words of a story that he would never forget.

"Let's see, here," he began. "'The Healing City, Chapter One; A Stranger Comes to Town'." There was the faintest catch in his voice as he continued.

"'...The story has been told and retold for more than thirty years now. And every time it's retold, it's been changed a bit. I've heard that the story happened in Australia, New Zealand, and England. Maybe something like this did happen in those places, but this is my story, so I'm here to tell you that it happened in my hometown. Where's that? It doesn't really matter. You probably never heard of it anyway. No one has. Although I didn't realize it at the time- none of us did- the story began one Christmas many years ago. The story began in the foothills of the Rockies when a *stranger arrived, unnoticed, in a small town not yet known as The Healing City'".*

CHAPTER ONE

A Stranger Comes to Town

Unnoticed. And that was the way he wanted it. For years now, everywhere he had gone, every move he had made was monitored by someone. Doctors, businessmen, secretaries, nurses, even preachers made note every time he crossed the street. Now only one man knew where he was, and Conrad Bernstein wasn't talking.

Stew Thomas looked like any other Ronan cowboy as he got off the bus early that October evening. Except that he looked more like a dime-store cowboy than he cared to admit, with his new jeans, flannel shirt, boots, and cowboy hat. But that couldn't be helped. His New York designer clothes would have made him even more out of place than he now felt. Not much more, however.

The biting cold air stung his exposed face and hands as he stepped off the bus and into the unfamiliar world of cowboys and Indians. What would his New York friends think if they saw him now? He knew the answer to that question.

At first no one believed him when he announced his decision to abandon his thriving medical practice for what they assumed was nothing more than an early mid-life crisis. But when his best friend started calling him Grizzly Adams, the high-priced doctors and nurses he spent his days and nights working with at New York Medical were willing to take his actions seriously. Over the last six months as he sold his home, traded in his Ferrari for a bus ticket, and re-assigned his patients to his partner, everyone was even more willing to acknowledge the seriousness of his decision, whether they accepted it or not.

Stew pulled the brim of his hat down in an attempt to protect his face from the wind and sleet, but it did little to ease the sting. Although it was still early evening, at least by New York standards, only an occasional cowboy braved the sidewalks. Most of the businesses along Main Street were already closed for the evening, some appearing to be closed permanently. The sun had retired for the night hours earlier, and the streetlights did little to quell the darkness of the night or the darkness of his soul. He tried not to think such dreary thoughts as he stepped away from the bus after taking his bag from the driver. The rest of his things, what he hadn't sold or given away months ago, would have already arrived at his new home. If you could call it that.

Conrad had taken charge of all the arrangements. Eight months earlier, Stew had started his subscription to the *Ronan Gazette*, and seven months ago he saw the ad for a veterinary clinic for sale. It seemed the local vet was getting on in years, and would rather retire than re-model and renovate his clinic to the new standards regulated by the state. So the building, equipment included, could be had at auction prices. While Stew was kept busy transferring his patients and his workload to his partner, Conrad had stepped in to handle his business affairs. And that included the purchase of the clinic, and the buying, selling, and trad-ing of medical equipment. Conrad had assured him that the purchase price, al-ready low, was an excellent deal consid-ering that the clinic was large enough for him to also use as living quarters, with a little additional remodeling and expense, of course.

As he stepped in the slush of yesterday's snow, he questioned whether he was walking in the right direction. Surely, if he could maneuver the streets of New York without getting lost, he could find one building on Main Street. East or West? North or South? He couldn't remember Conrad's directions so he just kept walking.

Glancing first to his right, then to his left, it was clear that whatever businesses there were in Ronan were all on this one street. Appropriately called Main Street, it appeared to be only about five or, at the most, six blocks long, with the small bus stop at the drug store in the center of town. If he was wrong, and the clinic was in the other direction, he wouldn't lose much time turning around at the end of Main Street and walking back in the other direction. Still, it was bitterly cold and he did not want to do any more walking than was absolutely necessary.

Shielding his eyes from the sleet, he saw only his boots as he forced himself to place one foot in front of the other and keep walking. Step. Step. Step. Had he not been forced to raise his eyes at the intersection, he would have missed his building.

His building. It sure didn't compare

to 'his building' in New York. Instead of lots of chrome, steel, and glass, there was an old paint-peeled, broken-windowed barn. At one time it had been painted a cheery red, but most of its three coats of paint had worn off years ago. The 'For Sale' sign still hung in the dirty, broken window, even though the former owner had mailed Stew the key more than a month ago. Apparently, life did indeed move at a slower--a much slower--pace in Montana.

No matter. Stew would enjoy the slower pace and the opportunity to get his hands dirty with remodeling. As a surgeon, that had not been a luxury afforded him for more years than he cared to remember.

Later he would take stock of the outside of his new building, but for now his primary--correction, his *only* concern, was to get inside and get warm. He knew that there would probably be no heat, but he would at least be out of the wind. Small comfort, but it was a comfort.

He was unable to reach his gloved hand into his jeans pocket for his keys, and was forced to remove his gloves with his teeth and try again for his keys. Looking at his hands, red and so cold they burned, he couldn't remember the last time he had been this cold. It must have been that winter when he was nine. The winter that he and Kevin spent sledding down the big hill behind the school house. That is, until they slid into the outside of the principal's office. The principal would have taken the sled away from him if it hadn't been smashed into so many pieces. That was one of the few times he remembered his father laughed at him, after he spanked him of course. Enough of that. Now he had to force his mind back to the task at hand.

As he slowly forced the frozen door open, the snow above the door fell on the brim of his hat and slid like melting icicles, stinging his eyes. He wiped his eyes with the back of his wet hands and cautiously stepped inside, checking along the wall for a light switch. The faint glow from the overhead light did little to improve his morale. He gave a low gasp as he looked around the foyer of what he hoped would some day be his clinic. Was he out of his mind? The room looked better in the dark. It wasn't the fact that the room was cluttered that bothered him. There was actually very little furniture in the room. It was the condition of the furnishings that disturbed him. As far as he could tell, every piece of furniture in the room was broken and useless.

That first night in Ronan, when he realized that he could not stay at his 'clinic', he found a room at The White Buffalo, the only hotel in town. Walking into the open foyer that first night, he did not need to ask where the name of the hotel came from. Aside from buffalo, deer, elk, and moose heads mounted on the walls, and a large bear rug on the floor, the only other decorations were framed newspaper stories about an albino buffalo that had lived at the nearby Moise Bison Range.

His room at The White Buffalo was clean, if a bit sparse. A single bed, a night table with a broken lamp, and a small dresser that the Salvation Army Thrift Store would have rejected were the room's only furnishings. He didn't realize until he lay down on the overly soft and well-used bed just how tired he was. Thoughts of New York streetlights, rushing yellow cabs, and assorted sirens mingled with the sounds of dogs barking as his head hit the pillow. His last conscious thoughts before sleep overtook his weary body that first night in Montana were of a small store front church with a slightly out of tune piano playing 'Just As I Am', while an old man with a half-empty bottle of Jack Daniels in his back pocket stood to testify of his love for Jesus.

He wasn't sure whether it was the smell of freshly brewed coffee or the rooster crowing his 'Good Morning World' that first reached his consciousness. Whatever it was, it wasn't the sounds of ambulances and police sirens that he had heard every morning for the past umpteen-odd years.

A quick bath and shave in the hall bathroom made him feel presentable enough to go in search of a daily paper, and maybe a cup of hot coffee in the lobby.

As he quickly read the paper (all twelve pages) he slowly read the people around him. Considering that one week earlier he had been performing high profile surgery in 'New York's finest', he was pleased with his new cowboy look, even if it was only a disguise. He knew that he blended into his surroundings, well, at least as long as he remembered to keep his mouth shut. As soon as he spoke, however, only a deaf man could think he was from Montana. No matter. He wasn't trying to hide the fact that he was from New York. He simply did not want that knowledge to prejudice the people of Ronan before they had a chance to get to know him personally.

As he skimmed the paper, not sure what he was expecting to find, or even what he was looking for, he observed those around him more closely. The man behind the counter was probably the owner. He was the same man on duty twelve hours earlier when Stew checked in. The lady who put the donuts and coffee on the long table against the back wall was probably his wife. Besides himself, the only other customers in The White Buffalo appeared to be two cowboys sitting at a table near the entrance, drinking coffee. From their conversation, he knew they were on their way from Kalispell to Missoula to pick up a few head of cattle, but stopped for the night due to the surprise snowstorm.

Three strong cups of coffee and two donuts later, he had finished the paper, collected his things, checked out of his room, and knew where he was going. The morning was surprisingly warm after yesterday's snow. Stew headed right on Main Street, down two doors from The White Buffalo, and into the Cattleman's Feed and Seed.

For a man used to scalpels, forceps, and syringes, it would take him awhile to get used to hammers, plungers, and sixteen-penny nails. Nevertheless, he was determined that his plan would work. He had no intentions of spending one more night at The White Buffalo, if he had a choice in the matter.

The friendly owner- manager-salesman-clerk spotted him as soon as he entered the store.

"Howdy, friend. Name's Burl. May I help you?"

"Uh, thanks. I'm new to town and I need to pick up a few things. I noticed the display in the window. The large per-colator, the blue one. And maybe a couple of these cast iron skillets."

"Anything else I can help you with?"

"Some information, maybe?"

"Shoot."

"Well, like I said, I'm new in town, and..."

"I'll be darned! You must be Stew Thomas. Glad to meet ya."

"How did you know...?"

"Now, don't get nervous on me. Ol' Bill Jacobs that runs The White Buffalo, well, his sister's married to my next-door neighbor. He was in here first thing this mornin' gettin' some chicken feed. He takes the donuts over to the hotel ever' mornin', at least ever' mornin' that there's guests at the hotel. Bill told him about you. Said you was real nice, but you talk kinda uppity. He didn't mean no disrespect by it, though, that's just his way. You gotta understand he ain't ever been more than a hundred miles from here his whole life, so he ain't never met a foreigner before."

"I'm not exactly a foreigner."

"Well, you sure ain't from Montana, are ya?"

"No, sir."

"Then you're a foreigner. Just what country are you from, anyway?"

"I most recently lived in New York, but I'm originally from..."

"New York, that's what I thought. I could tell right away you wasn't from around here. Well, friend, let me be the first to welcome you to God's country. Now, what's that information you're wanting?"

"I can get some of the supplies I need from your store, but I'm also going to need some plumbing..."

"Got it."

"Supplies. And some lumber, and..."

"Got it."

"Lots of paint."

"That it?"

"It's a start. I'm sure I'll need more supplies as soon as I take inventory of my new clinic."

"Oh, so you're the new vet that took over for Doc Holland."

"Uh, no. I'm a doctor."

"That's what I said. Doc Holland sure was a good vet. Fact is, he delivered most of the babies in Ronan for the last thirty years. Too bad, 'bout them new regulations on your building. I think maybe it would be easier to tear the whole thing down and start over than it will be to remodel. Tell you what. How 'bout you just give me a list of what you need? Then go on over next door to The Lazy B, that's the diner. My wife, Jean, she runs it. Tell her to give you a piece of her famous rhubarb pie. By the time you're done with your pie I'll have everything ready for you to pick up. I didn't notice a truck outside, you want me to deliver it?"

"Thank you; that would be very nice. By the way, do you know where I could get a good used car around here? I came in on the bus yesterday and it was dark when I got here. I walked around a little this morning, but I don't remember seeing a car lot close by."

"There ain't one. Nearest car lot is in Polson, and that's a pretty good walk from here. But if you go down Main Street two more blocks and turn left at the old library, then past the old church on your left, you'll see the John Deere lot. It's run by Jimmy Scott. He sometimes has used cars available. Check there first. But let me tell ya', if you're plannin' on using that car to get around these mountains, you better make sure that car's a truck."

"John Deere. Got it. Thanks again. I really appreciate all your help."

"Don't think nothin' 'bout it. Just tryin' to be neighborly."

"If you don't mind, I'll go ahead and check on that truck after I stop at The Lazy B. I should be back in about an hour."

"See you then. I'll have everything packed up for you. If I think of anything else I figure you'll need, I'll just put it in the box. You can pay me when I deliver it, or I'll bill you, whichever you prefer."

"I'll pay you when you deliver it. I don't like bills hanging over my head."

"None of us do, Mister, but sometimes you just gotta hold on and hope you don't go down for the third time." Stew's head began to hurt as he tried to figure out that last statement.

He was still thinking about old pickup trucks as he stepped up to the counter of The Lazy B and reconsidered ordering his first piece of rhubarb pie. Oh, what the heck, he thought. When in Montana, eat like the Montanans. Or something like that.

He was surprised at how hungry he actually was, and how good the pie actually tasted. Looking at his watch, he realized he had better hurry to the John Deere lot if he was going to find a truck and get back to the Feed and Seed within the hour.

It wasn't hard to find the John Deere lot, since there was only one in town. In fact, there was probably only one of anything in Ronan. As for choosing the right pickup, that was also pretty easy. There was only one on the lot. The dealer said it was old, but had only had one owner. He had traded it in on a new tractor just before harvest. With a promise to deliver the part-time car dealer's next calf and three hundred dollars less in his wallet, Stew drove off the lot in his new--well, new to him--1946 Dodge Power Wagon.

Behind the wheel of his new Power Wagon, he was beginning to feel like he might someday fit in with the locals. True, he would never be a cowboy, but maybe he wouldn't look so much like a New York foreigner either.

He pulled into the small back parking lot of the clinic just as Burl was unloading his last box of supplies in the front waiting room. Until right then, Stew had not thought about the fact that he had forgotten to give Burl a key.

"Hey, Burl, thanks again for delivering my things, but how did you get in? I forgot to give you a key."

"That's okay, the lock was broken anyway. Just one more thing you'll need to fix. After I close up shop today I'll bring you over a new lock. I don't have the fancy ones like you use on them penthouses in New York, but I reckon it'll do the trick. Most folks around here don't lock their doors anyway, unless they got money hid somewhere, and if they got money they prob'ly don't live here anyway. Noticed you got yourself a new truck. Hate to tell you, but it sure looks like it's been rode hard and put away wet."

"I'll admit it's no Ferrari, but I'm sure it will get me around town all right. How much do I owe you?"

"Fifty dollars and we'll call it even."

"You sure?"

"Sure enough. Folks around here treat their vets well, even if they are only people doctors."

Within the hour, his assortment of new tools were lying on the counter as if he was preparing for surgery, while two cans of paint were opened on the floor, and the broken and useless furniture had been loaded into the back of his Wagon for a trip tomorrow morning to the dump.

He decided that the smallest exam

room would be the easiest to heat, so after sweeping out the dust, garbage, and remnants of peeled wallpaper, he set up his portable heater and cot in the corner farthest from the drafty window. It didn't look much like his New York apartment, but it would do. Temporarily.

———

The next three weeks were a blur of activity. And inactivity. As he worked, maybe harder than he ever had in surgery, he tried to sort out both his thoughts and his feelings.

Over the next three weeks, Stew built and cleaned and repaired and cleaned and remodeled and cleaned and tore out and cleaned and put in and cleaned, and when he was all done, just for good measure he cleaned some more. The work may have been rough on his hands, but it was good for his mind. It gave him the opportunity to reevaluate where he was, and what he was doing.

If a man can have culture shock without leaving his own culture, well then, Stew Thomas had culture shock. Big time. He had given up more than just money in moving to Montana. He had given up his life as he knew it. And he knew that few, if any, would understand his reasons. After all, he reminded himself, he had given up in order to move to Montana what most Montanans were leaving Montana to find! Money, fame, and the most promising of futures, that's what he left behind. A drafty old barn, sick cows, and an old truck with one head light; that was his new life.

So why do it? He asked himself that question for the umpteen millionth time. His answer was the same as it had always been. He did not have to prove to himself, or anyone else, for that matter, that he could be a success. He had already done that. Neither did he have to prove to himself that he could be a cowboy. He doubted he could ever be as comfortable in a cowboy hat and boots as he was in a lab coat. Still, in his heart, he did have something to prove. A voice from his past wanted him to cling to the belief that he had to prove to himself that he could be a man, a real man. Not a doctor, or a cowboy, but a man. And that voice from his past, that voice from twenty years ago, wanted to convince him that the measure of a man is not what he takes, but what he gives. Not what he says or even what he does, but what he is.

There were other voices in his mind as well. Stronger voices. Voices he had learned to recognize and listen to. Voices that daily reminded him it was time to set in motion his plan. But to do that, he had to start over somewhere that no one knew who he was. As far from New York as possible. Somewhere that time wasn't measured primarily by clocks and calendars, but by growing seasons and family outings. Somewhere like Montana. So he had sold what he could sell, and given away what he couldn't sell. He knew that he could take his investments, buy himself a small cabin, and live comfortably for many years to come. If he wanted to. But that wasn't his plan.

Pouring himself a strong cup of coffee, he sat down on a small wooden crate and reviewed his plan. He remembered almost dismissing the plan as soon as it entered his mind. What a foolish idea it was, after all, to throw away the career of a lifetime! But the more he had tried to forget his plan, the stronger it became in his mind, until it could no longer be ignored. Over the past seven months, the plan had grown to almost overpowering proportions. Was it an obsession? He didn't know. He only knew that he no longer had a choice. He had to put the plan in action. And he had to do it now.

His plan of action had been scary at first, he admitted to himself, but at least it was simple. With another sip of coffee, he stretched out his long legs and put his well-trained mind into 'analyze' mode. The first step was completed. He was in Montana and was beginning to get his new clinic in some sort of order. It was far from completed, but it was at least started.

The next step of the plan was crucial, maybe the most crucial part of all. He would get to know the people of Ronan without letting the people of Ronan get to know him. Oh, they would know him as a doctor. And they would know he was from New York. Some people might even go so far as to learn that he used to be in the ministry, but beyond that, his life would be a mystery. It was imperative, for the plan to work, that no one ever learn his true reason for moving to Ronan. If even one person knew his reason for leaving New York, his plan would be a failure. He would be a failure. He would never lie to anyone, he told himself, since it was too hard to keep track of lies, but he would not divulge any information that was not necessary to his purpose. Yes, he reminded himself, step two was to keep his life a mystery without letting anyone know he was keeping his life a mystery. Only with the firm foundation of steps one and two in place could he begin step three. And by the time step three was accomplished the people of Ronan would believe that Stew Thomas was indispensable, or at least irreplaceable in their lives.

The knock on the front door jolted his mind back to the present. Consciously wiping the smirk off his face, he slowly stood and headed toward the door that opened before he reached it.

"Howdy, Friend. 'Member me?"

"Hello, uh, howdy, yourself. Burl, isn't it?"

"Yup, sir. Just thought I'd stop by and see how you was doing. Are you needing any more supplies?"

"I've been making a list. I thought I might stop by later this week, after I got a little more of the remodeling done."

"Noticed you don't have your vet's sign out front yet. Don't know how people are gonna know you're open for business without a sign."

"As I said before, I'm not a vet, I'm a doctor. And I'm a long ways from ready for any business."

"Couldn't help but notice your stack of magazines. Don't know why you need those in here. Cows can't read."

"Mr., uh, Burl, I really am busy. As you can see, I have a lot of work to do before I'm ready to hang my 'Open For

Business' sign in the window. Is there something specific I can do for you before I get back to work?"

"No. Just being neighborly. You know, for a foreigner, you ain't too bad of a carpenter. Your place is looking pretty good."

"Thanks. I appreciate that. You're the first person that's come by to see the place since I started working on it."

"Trust me, I won't be the last. The whole town's excited about having the vet's shop open again. I reckon the vet's about the most important man in these parts, maybe even more important than the owner of the Feed and Seed, if you can believe the way people talk. And speaking of the Feed and Seed, I better get back to work. I ain't got anyone minding the store. I just left a note in the window that I was coming over here to visit for a minute and I'd be right back. Folk's 'll be askin' me how you're doing over here, and I need to be able to tell 'em first hand that the vet's shop 'll be open any day now."

"It will still be a few more weeks before the clinic will be open, but if anyone wants to stop by and get acquainted, I'll enjoy the company and it will give me a chance to get to know the people I'm here to serve."

"I'll be sure to pass the word along.

Like I said, everyone's anxious to get the vet's shop open again. By the way, I noticed you still have that old furnace of Doc Holland's. That thing didn't heat up this place even when it was new. I've got a nice furnace in stock that'll be better for ya. You'll want to put it in before you get your remodelin' done, 'cuz you'll prob'ly have to do some wall cuttin' to get it in here. Keep that in mind."

"I'll do that. Thanks again, for stopping by."

"Oh, I almost forgot. My wife Jean, she noticed how much you enjoyed her rhubarb pie, so she had me bring you a jar of her rhubarb sauce. It's almost as famous as her rhubarb pie."

"Tell her 'thank you' for me. And I'll be in later this week with a new supplies order."

"Gotcha, Friend. Be seein' ya."

As Burl returned to his Feed and Seed, Stew had the distinct impression that Burl would be a man of his word, and it would only be a matter of time before everyone in Ronan came by to give him a piece of advice and find out for themselves how soon the clinic would be open for business. Cultivating a friendship with Burl might just be the most important aspect of step three in his plan to change the lives of the good people of

Ronan.

CHAPTER TWO

The Doctor and the Lady

And so it went. Burl was indeed a man of his word. In a matter of days, Stew had stopped counting all the people who had stopped by the clinic to wish him well and give him neighborly advice as to all the reasons his clinic could not work.

It was during the bursts of inactivity, such as when he was waiting for paint to dry, that he set about to establish the routine he would follow, at least until his clinic was finally open for business. He had already spent two days with a note-pad in hand, organizing his thoughts on paper. As he reviewed his notes he wondered if this much planning went into the organization of a bank robbery. His outline was clear, concise, and consistent.

Item #1: Eat breakfast every day at the White Buffalo. The other guests would all assume I had spent the night there also, and since they would assume they would never see me again, they would be willing to talk and give me information about news in the surrounding area.

Item #2: Eat lunch every day at the diner. Always eat at the same time. Become a regular. People will get used to seeing me and won't be as suspicious of me. The friendlier I am to them, the easier it will be for them to be friendly to me. Do everything I can to get them to tell me about themselves without my telling them anything about me.

Item #3: Visit as many stores in town as possible. Again, make sure people think of me as a regular. People aren't suspicious of you at Jake's Grocery and Tackle Shop.

Item #4: Research at the libr—no, make that the cemetery. If I look up town history at the library, people may see me and question what I'm up to. At the cemetery I may find the information I need without anyone questioning me.

Item #5: Always carry a Bible with me. It's very important for people to see me as sincere and religious. (Those years in the ministry should at least pay off. I know the 'language' and I can hold my own in any Bible discussion.)

There were, of course, more items on

the list, but that was enough to think about for the moment. For now, he had to get back to work. Setting the notepad on the counter next to his watch, he climbed the ladder to check the paint on the ceiling. If it was dry, he would be able to hang the new light fixture before lunch. His finger almost reached the ceiling just as the bell above the front door chimed. Didn't anyone pay attention to his 'Not Quite Open Yet' sign in the window? Maybe if he just kept working, they would see how busy he was and leave. No such luck. Out of the corner of his eye he could see the woman, maybe a little older than he was, and the boy, probably her son, enter the room and cross over to just below where he was standing on the ladder. The boy was holding his arm. He tried to sound busy as he explained a little too loudly, "If you're here with supplies, then just put them on the counter. Otherwise the list is tacked to the door. Just sign your name and reason on the way out."

"Please, my son's hurt!"

In one swift move he was down the ladder, had slipped on his watch, and was giving a cursory examination of the boy. "Excuse me, ma'am. What have we got here?" It didn't look like much more than a few scrapes and bruises. Mothers panic too easily, he reminded himself. The best hypochondriacs have always been women.

The boy's embarrassment at least matched his pain. "It's nuthin'. Mom's just fussin'. I got throwed again is all. That Thunder's just too wild for me. I can't even stay on him long enough to get bucked off. It seems like all he has to do is snort too loudly and I fall off. Only thing that's really hurt is my pride."

Being a professional man, Stew did not let the mother or son see his grin as he turned away to look for some bandages he thought he had put under the counter. While he used his most doctorish voice, he continued to look through boxes on the counter. "Well, you did right by coming in, but as you can see I'm not ready for business. It'll take me a minute to find my first aid supplies."

The woman's smile matched his. "I believe, doctor, that your bag is right there on the counter."

Now it was his turn to be embarrassed. "Uh, thanks." As he stretched his left arm across the counter to reach his bag, his watchband caught the corner of a box top and forced the box to come crashing down, spilling first aid supplies on the floor. Momentarily forgetting the boy's cuts and scrapes, which after all were only superficial, he scrambled through the medical supplies to recover his watch, but not before the mother noticed the tattoo on his left wrist where his watch had been.

As Stew replaced his watch, the mother's experienced eyes saw the bandages and ointment she needed to cover her son's scrapes and cuts. Did he hear a smile on her face as she addressed him?

"I realize, doctor, that you're just moving to town. But, well, for a doctor you don't seem very organized. Are you sure you went to medical school?"

Yes, he was certain that was a smile on her face as she looked around his almost-just-barely organized office.

"New York's finest. And if you'll pardon me for saying so, ma'am, for a 'lay-person'..."

"Good word choice."

"You're pretty good with a band-aid."

"Well, you can't be a mom for twenty years without knowing a few things about band-aids."

"Your husband must be proud."

"I'm widowed."

Great, Stew, he rebuked himself. *So much for your bedside manner. Where do I sign up for that course on winning friends and influencing people? This is not going to help step two of my plan one little bit.* He hoped he sounded sincere when he found his voice. "I'm sorry. I didn't mean to..."

There was a barely discernible quiver in her voice as she spoke. Each sentence was a story of its own. "It's all right. You didn't know. It's been twenty years."

Stew had regained his composure enough to sound sincere. "I'm sorry. It must be tough."

"Tough?" the boy asked. "Let me tell you, she's the toughest dad a boy ever had." As the boy spoke again, Stew realized that this wasn't a boy at all, but a 'young man fully grown'. At least, that's what Stew's father would have said. Funny, Stew thought, how you can remember the strangest things for no apparent reason.

The mother smiled as if this were a private joke between the two of them. "That's right, son. And don't you forget it. Say, Doctor..."

"Stewart. Stewart Thomas. But just call me Stew. Doctor Thomas sounds too formal for a Montana doctor."

"Stew it is, then. I'm Marcie Stone. And this is my son, Joey."

"Howdy, Stew." Some could see the boy's face as young, but his handshake was that of an adult.

"Howdy right back at ya."

"Thanks for patching me up, Doc. I appreciate it."

"You're welcome, but it was your mom that did all the work."

"I know. I just wanted to make you feel good. I make her feel good all the time." They all laughed, and it felt good.

After a moment Marcie continued the discussion. "You said, Doctor--I mean Stew--that you went to medical school in New York. What brings you to a one-horse town in Montana? We don't even have paved streets."

Stew was already prepared for the question. He had rehearsed his answer numerous times before today. "That's why I came. A man can only take so much of a big city before he goes crazy." He paused for effect before continuing. "I wanted to leave before that happened to me. Most of my friends told me that coming to Montana was proof I'd already gone crazy. But looking around, I'm not sure this is a one-horse town. There are more horses within a hundred miles than there are people. I'm thinking I'd make more money if I was a vet. And to hear Burl at the Feed and Seed tell it, the rest of the town thinks so too."

Marcie appreciated Stew's sense of humor, and she hoped he knew what he was getting himself into. "That's probably true. To be honest, I don't know if Ronan, Montana, can keep a doctor in business. We had the only hospital between Missoula and Kalispell, and it was forced to close a couple years ago. Just wasn't enough need to keep up with the expenses."

Stew sensed that Marcie liked him. He also knew that a little humor goes a long way in making someone comfortable about sharing details of their life. "I tell you, as long as Joey keeps old Thunder around, I'll stay in business." He laughed at his own joke, and then when Marcie and Joey also laughed he spoke quietly, as if divulging a great secret. He chose his next words with the same care that he chose his instruments for surgery. "But the truth is, I didn't come here for the money. I don't expect it will cost me much to live here."

Joey surveyed the room as if seeing it for the first time. "Are you planning on living in this barn, along with setting up shop here? That's just plain crazy!"

Marcie's look stopped him before her words did. "Joey! That was rude! Where did you learn to talk like that?"

Joey didn't mean to become defensive. The words came out before he thought them through. "Well, it's the truth."

Marcie's tone matched that of her son. "I know, but it's still rude."

Joey's face was crestfallen. As if he was a five- year-old with his hand caught in the cookie jar. "I'm sorry."

Stew hoped his expression was as sincere as his words. "Apology accepted."

Marcie could see that Stew had thought his plans through, but she still felt obligated to warn him of what may lay ahead. "Stew, I don't want to dampen your spirits any, but Joey's right. Our winters here are really rough. This old barn is drafty at best. Besides, it'll be expensive to repair, let alone heat."

This is where I reel them in, Stew thought. It's time to put step three in place. "I don't mind the expense. Money's not a problem. I did well in New York. I'm not rich, even by Montana standards, but I have some money put aside."

Joey's face, even more than his words, let Stew know he was getting the response he was looking for. Joey bit the worm. "It can't be enough to repair this old..."

Marcie's eyes flashed. "Joey!"

"Sorry."

Stew knew it was time to sound like a concerned father. "That's okay. Truth is, I have enough money to live on for quite awhile. I have some investments back in

New York that will keep me going. I know people here don't have much money. I have a couple ideas of how to help them. First, I'm not going to charge them for my services."

Marcie couldn't help her reaction. "That's crazy!"

And Joey couldn't help taking advantage. "Mother!"

Now it was Marcie who had her hand in the cookie jar. "Sorry. Now I know where Joey learned it." She hoped she didn't sound too motherly as she continued. "But Stew, you need to know something about these people. The Indians that live here on the reservation have a rich heritage on this land. Their families have been here for hundreds of years. And as for the cowboys, let's just say Montana cowboys don't have a shortage of pride. They don't take charity, no matter how much they may need it at times. They won't respect you if they think you feel sorry for them."

Stew's answer was measured, as if every word counted. "What do you suggest, then? I don't want to take their money when I don't need it, and I know how hard it is to come by."

Marcie's eyes sparkled like when she was in the third grade and was the only student that knew the answer to the question the teacher had put on board. "Let the people pay you in kind."

"What do you mean?"

"Well, I see it like this. The ranchers don't have much money, but they have cattle or sheep. Even the people that live in town have chickens. And everyone has a garden. They can keep your pantry full all winter."

"That sounds like a good idea. That is, if I ever get to put it in practice, no pun intended."

Joey wasn't sure he was following the conversation. "What do you mean, Doc?"

Stew sounded like he did when he was explaining a tonsillectomy to a five–year-old. "Remember what I said to you when you first came in?"

"About putting supplies on the counter? We didn't bring any supplies."

"No, I mean this." He stepped to the front door and pulled the note off the window where he had taped it a couple weeks ago. "I've been working here day and night for almost three weeks. In that time, I think everyone in town has stopped by. Except they didn't come for my excellent medical care. Everyone had their own story about how and why I was foolish to try and open a clinic here. I finally got so tired of it that I just put up the note and told people to fill it in on their way out the door. Figured it would make them happy and stop me wasting so much time jabbering when I could be working."

Joey read the list slowly, savoring every word. "It's a mighty formidable list."

"Formidable." Stew said the word as if it were the most holy word ever spoken. "Now that's a good word for it. You should be a writer, Joey."

Joey's eyes shined like his mother's. "That's what I want to be. At least writing doesn't land me on my keester in the mud."

"Go for it, then."

Joey quickly lost the shine in his eyes. "Nah. I'm only a Montana cowboy. I couldn't write anything anyone would want to read."

"If you give up that easily, maybe you're right."

Stew was surprised at how quickly Joey's eyes went from shining to flaming. Joey was trying to hold his feelings in check, but he wasn't succeeding. "Doc, that's not fair. You don't even know me, to talk to me like that."

Stew knew he could not afford to smile, no matter how badly he wanted to. "Then prove me wrong."

Joey could barely speak through

tears of anger and pain. "I will! Now, if you'll excuse me, I've got a horse to break. Thanks," he paused for effect, "Mom, for patching me up." He handed Stew back his list before he or Marcie could think of an appropriate response. Joey made sure the door slammed behind him on his way out. Marcie was the first to speak.

"You did that on purpose, didn't you?"

Stew drawled in his best John Wayne fashion. "A man's gotta do what a man's gotta do." He lowered his voice as he finished his thought. "Now let's just see if it works. But he's right about one thing. This is a formidable list. A lot of good reasons why this can't work."

The sparkle returned quickly to Marcie's eyes. Stew decided they were green. Or maybe blue. "Well, if you give up that easily, maybe they're right."

He didn't even pretend to hide his laugh. "Are all the people in this town as tough as you?"

"Nope. Only the men. Now, you said you had a couple ideas of how to help these people, but so far you've only mentioned one. What else are you thinking?"

Before he answered her, he reached out and grabbed two straight-back chairs and set them back to back. He leaned into his chair as he let it stand on its two back legs, noticing that she sat more lady-like in her chair. Green. Her eyes were definitely green. This was the moment he had been waiting for, but how much should he say? He knew it was imperative that she see him as sincere. He hoped she did not notice that he was sweating. He remembered something he had heard from his speech professor in college. Something like 'when you are nervous, speak slowly. It will make you sound more authoritative and your audience will tend to believe you even if you are lying through your teeth'. He hoped it was true, and he was about to find out whether his tuition was worth it. Stew took a long, deep breath before he began.

"Like I said, I have some investments back in New York that are doing well. A long time ago a-uh-an anonymous benefactor helped me out without knowing it at the time. Because of what he did for me, I went into medicine in the first place. I want to return the favor and set up a fund, anonymously, to help the people of Ronan. The money will be used to help people in emergencies. It will be kind of like having a financial clinic along with my medical clinic, to help meet the needs of both the body and the soul. Maybe it could be used to help out farmers during times of drought or flood or whatever it is that destroys crops around here. I've read enough *Little House on the Prairie* books to know you can't have a good crop every year." He had only one thought: *Did she buy it?*

"That sounds great, but like I said, the people won't accept charity if..."

"Now, don't get me wrong" he hurried. "It's not charity, here. There are two conditions behind every financial gift."

Marcie sounded suspicious. "What conditions?"

"Everyone that receives a gift must agree to two things. First, they must accept that it is a gift given in the name of Jesus Christ, and second, as soon as their own emergency is over, they must find someone else to bless, anonymously, of course. There is a Bible principle here. Let me show you." He continued to speak as he rummaged through the stack of boxes nearest the counter. "My study Bible isn't unpacked yet, but I have an easy to read devotional Bible here that I keep in my waiting room. Here it is." He quickly turned to the page he was looking for, all the while hoping that the presence of the Bible would give him the needed credibility he sought.

His practice as a one-time preacher came in handy as he spoke. "This is from 2Corinthians 1:3-4. It says, 'What a wonderful God we have- he is the Father of our Lord Jesus Christ, the source of every mercy, and the one who so wonderfully comforts and strengthens us in our hardships and trials. And why does he do this? So that when others are troubled, needing our sympathy and encouragement, we can pass on to them this same help and comfort God has given us.'"

Marcie noticed that he was getting more excited as he spoke. She wondered to herself whether or not he had ever thought of going into the ministry. She smiled to encourage him as he continued.

"And let me show you something else in chapter nine. It says here, 'A farmer who plants just a few seeds will get only a small crop, but if he plants much, he will reap much.' Now, let me skip down a few verses. And here it says, 'God is able to make it up to you by giving you everything you need and more, so that there will not only be enough for your own needs, but plenty left over to give joyfully to others. It is as the Scriptures say: 'The godly man gives generously to the poor. His good deeds will be an honor to him forever.' For God, who gives seed to the farmer to plant, and later on, good crops to harvest and eat, will give you more and more seed to plant and will make it grow so that you can give away more and more fruit from your harvest. Yes, God will give you much so that you can give away much, and when we take your gifts to those who need them they will break out into thanksgiving and praise to God for your help. So, two good things happen as a result of your gifts- those in need are helped, and they overflow with thanks to God. Those you help will be glad, not only because of your generous gifts to themselves and to others, but they will praise God for this proof that your deeds are as good as your doctrine. And they will pray for you with deep fervor and feeling because of the wonderful grace of God shown through you.' Do you see the principle?"

She was overwhelmed. By what, he could not tell. "I think so, but I'm not sure."

He explained slowly, carefully. "It's simple. First, we need to understand that every trial we go through is so that we can somehow use that trial to bless others. And second, that the more we bless others, the more God blesses us so that we can continue to bless others. It's a never-ending cycle, like skipping pebbles on the water. The ripple effect just keeps going." The preacher-actor-doctor pretended to be stern. "Now, Miss Marcie, because I have revealed my true mission in life to you, I must swear you to secrecy."

"You mean your mission in life is to be a bad actor?"

Sincerity, he thought. She must not only see it on my face, she must feel it coming from deep inside me. He brushed away a tear she did not see. "My mission in life is to be a healer. But not just a doctor. That is only my cover. I pretend to be a mild-mannered doctor in order to sneak in undercover. Then, when I'm certain no one is looking, I transform myself into 'The Healer', mender of broken bones and broken hearts. Think of it, Marcie. If every time God blessed us or met our needs, we, in turn, would use that blessing to meet the needs of others, anonymously, of course. Think of what that would mean to those around us. It could change the whole city. We could go from the meek and mild 'Ronan' to 'The Healing City'. And there's no reason for it to stop there. Why, I want to share God's blessings so much that I may start praying for a few more disasters around here, just so I can show people the blessings of God."

This was a lot for her to take in. There was more to Stew Thomas than met the eye. Of course, even the part that met the eye wasn't too hard to look at. "Stew Thomas, you may not be much of a cowboy, but you're certainly a character."

"Guilty as charged, Ma'am."

"Oh, you're guilty all right. I'm just not sure of what it is that you're guilty of. But seriously, I do see one thing on this list you need to think about, and real soon."

Stew tried to remember everything that was written on the list. "What's that?"

"This building is drafty, and the worst of winter is not far away. Here in the mountains it can sneak up on you over-night. Even if you were to work around the clock, you couldn't make this place both a home and a clinic before the seri-ous snow comes. And if you try, then you'll need a doctor yourself before long. Then where will the town be?"

"What do you suggest? I have a little money, but I don't want to buy an-other..."

Marcie was quick to interrupt. "I'm not suggesting you buy anything. I have a little rooming house. It isn't fancy, but it's warm, the cooking's good, and most of the guests are at least tolerable."

"You sure know how to make an at-tractive offer, but like I said, I really don't want to pay..."

"I'm not talking about paying. I'll make you the same deal you're giving the town. You just keep bandaging up Joey, and every Saturday I'll keep you full of the best fried chicken and apple pie you can eat. What do you say, Doc?" With that, she extended her hand for him to shake.

Shaking hands, he knew that step three was going to be even easier than he had hoped. "I say I got me a new land-lady. And I'll be the judge of your fried chicken and apple pie. But I do have one question. If I stay at your place, what'll I do with all the home-canned goods the ranchers pay me with?"

"Marcie's boarding house can always use more groceries."

"If I didn't know any better," he laughed, "I'd say you planned it this way. Lead the way, I'm getting hungry." As he reached under the counter for his homemade 'Not quite open yet' sign to put in the window he thought to himself, *This is going to be so easy.*

CHAPTER THREE

Stoneheart Inn

As Marcie silently prepared herself for bed she reflected again on the events of the day. What was it about Dr. Thomas that caused her mind to reel back in time? She knew the answer without hesitation. It had happened so quickly that maybe she didn't really see it. No, she couldn't fool herself any more--she had seen it, the mark on his wrist. The mark he had tried unsuccessfully to hide with his watchband.

True, she had never seen that kind of mark on anyone before, but she had heard the stories, especially from the old-timers around town. The mark could only mean one thing.

But what did that prove, really? He had the mark, so what? So some part of Dr. Stewart Thomas was a lie, or at least a secret, that's what. And didn't every-

one--even Marcie--have a right to their own little secrets? It would be a long time before Marcie fell asleep that night.

———

Stew couldn't believe his good luck as he unloaded his final box of personal items in his new room at Marcie's boarding house. Even its name, *Stoneheart Inn,* seemed to fit into his plans for the little town.

That first evening, even before he had brought over his first box from the clinic, he had managed to convince Marcie to invite Burl to dinner. In fact, he congratulated himself, he had even convinced Marcie that it was her idea in the first place. As he had suspected, it wasn't necessary for him to say much over that first night's dinner of buffalo steaks, mashed potatoes, fresh homemade bread, salad and cherry cobbler. Burl fit right in with the rest of Marcie's roomers, and before the mashed potatoes were cold Marcie had bragged to Burl about Stew's plans to 'help the city financially as the city learned to help others less fortunate than themselves.' Of course, it went without saying that the help from the city would be given by way of the good doctor. By Sunday afternoon, he figured, the whole town would be talking about how great it was to have Doctor Stewart Thomas and his new clinic 'for their very own'. He silently laughed to himself as he realized that 'the good doctor' had won over the town without having to fire a 'shot'.

As he laid out his toiletries on top of his dresser, he analyzed the personalities of each of the other roomers. First, there was Elizabeth, Marcie's mother. If anyone was a perfect 'Aunt Bee' it was Elizabeth. So much like his own mother, he thought. He must not dwell on that, he chastened himself, and forced the next name to come to mind. Joey. He seemed like a good kid. Hard working, honest, shy. Whether or not Joey would ever become a writer, Stew wasn't sure, but he was certain that Joey had what it took to make something of himself. Someday, Joey would make his mother proud.

Stew didn't exactly dislike Buck, but he couldn't honestly say that he liked him, either. Something about Buck was phony, that's all there was to it. And Stew understood about phonies.

In a word, Murphy, or 'Miss Murphy' as everyone called her, was a non-entity. For all practical purposes she was invisible. In twenty years she would be exactly the same person she was today, only grayer.

And last there was Marcie. Now, he could spend a lot of time analyzing her, and enjoying every minute of it, but he knew that it was almost suppertime.

He quietly closed the bedroom door behind him and started down the hallway, smelling supper cooking in the kitchen. When he heard the conversation in the living room, he realized that it would be advantageous to not let his presence be known quite yet.

Stepping into the hall bath, he left the door slightly ajar and turned the faucet on as low as possible, to still hear the conversations from the living room while giving him an 'out' in case he was caught. He had never spent as much time washing his hands before surgery as he now spent washing them for Elizabeth's fried chicken and apple pie.

Although he could not see the occupants of the living room, he could clearly picture each of them in his mind. Joey would be seated at the small desk to the left of the fireplace, writing in his journal. The other side of the fireplace was filled with a large Christmas tree, still undecorated. Miss Murphy would be playing checkers, by herself, most likely, at the card table to the right of the picture window. Buck would be pretending to not notice Miss Murphy as he read his Zane Grey western. Marcie and Elizabeth would be running errands back and forth from the kitchen to the dining room, with periodic stops in the living room to check on everyone and make sure they were ready for supper.

Stew could hear Marcie's footsteps, then the swinging door opening from the dining room to the living room as she spoke. "What do you think, everyone, is this the year we finally ..."

He guessed that Buck didn't even look up as he finished Marcie's sentence for her. "...replace the old star on the top of the tree, or will it do for one more year?" The laughter from the others was all the encouragement Buck needed to continue. "Marcie, you have asked that question every Christmas since you've had this place. I don't see that it matters. No one but us is ever going to see the tree, and we know what the stupid star looks like. And none of us cares. The star will be fine for another year." The room was suddenly unbearably quiet.

The swinging door opened again. Slower footsteps. It must be Elizabeth. "Dinner's almost ready. About another twenty minutes." The door swung shut behind her before Stew heard Buck's gruff voice.

"I don't see why she has to do that every night. Dinner has been the same time every night for twenty years."

Marcie's voice was almost too soft for Stew to hear over the running water. "My, aren't we in a good mood tonight."

Buck made no pretense at hiding his sarcasm. "Sorry."

As Miss Murphy spoke, Stew wondered if she always acted as a go-between. "You know it's just her way. It makes her feel special. Like she's important."

Buck's superiority was obvious. "She's just a cook, for goodness' sake."

Stew could tell that Marcie was used to handling Buck. He wondered if her eyes were lit up as she spoke. "She's not just a cook. She's my mother, and she is important to us. You don't look like her cooking has hurt you any." Again, the silence.

Miss Murphy, the go-between, was the first to speak. "Come on, Buck, it's almost Christmas. If you don't start being nice, Santa won't bring you anything. Why don't you play checkers with me until dinner? It's no fun playing myself. I always lose."

Buck's tone was as close to apologetic as Stew thought he was capable of. "Oh, all right. I'm not going to get this book read with all this jabbering going on anyway."

Joey finally entered the conversation. "You've read that book four times already. You should have the ending memorized by now. I would think you could find something more interesting to do with your time than re-read the same book over and over."

Buck was more than just irritated, he was angry. "Hey, Greenhorn, Zane Grey's a classic! And you're a fine one to talk. All you ever do is write in that stupid diary of yours. At least Zane Grey's good writing."

Joey may not have been pouting, but he was close. "It's not a diary, it's a journal."

Buck may not have been the king of wit, but was certainly the king of sarcasm. "And the difference, Greenhorn, is?"

Stew's hands were beginning to wrinkle under the steady stream, and he needed to think about a way to discreetly cross to the living room as Marcie's voice stopped him. "All right, you two!"

Miss Go-between once again attempted to change the subject. "Say, shouldn't someone go get Doc Stewart? He may not remember when dinner is." That was his cue. He turned off the water, closed the door behind him and started to walk down the hall when Buck's voice stopped him. "Are you volunteering?"

Stew knew that the conversation was about to take a change in direction, and that if he entered the living room now, all talking would cease. Quickly, he opened the hall closet door and began rummaging through the towels and washcloths, hoping that if he was caught he would at least look natural. From his new vantage point, he could see into the living room but no one could see him without making a serious effort to change the direction of their gazes. He could see Miss Murphy's lower lip quiver as she spoke. "I only meant that..."

"We all know what you meant. Come on, it's your move."

Stew was impressed with how easily Marcie was able to continually turn the conversation to friendlier subjects. Although he could see that her face showed the tension of the moment, her voice was calm and almost sweet. "I think it'll be nice having a real doctor in town again. Especially since everyone's predicting a hard winter."

Joey's laugh was good-natured. "Mom, this is Montana. Have you ever seen a 'good' winter?"

"Not recently. It will be nice to not have to go all the way to Missoula or Kalispell for a doctor in an emergency."

Buck, the resident pessimist, could not miss the opportunity to be negative. "I don't know. I stopped in on that new clinic of his--doesn't look like much of an operation to me." Only Buck laughed at his attempt at humor. Come to think of it, Stew thought, I don't remember Buck ever coming into the clinic when I was working. Then, choosing to give Buck the benefit of the doubt, he considered that maybe he had come into the shop on one of Stew's many trips to Burl's Feed and Seed. Anyway, the thought made Stew realize that he needed to stay aware of anything Buck said or did. A little bit of suspicion seemed healthy under the circumstances.

Miss Murphy was quick to defend Stew. "He's just getting started," she said. "At least let him get his clinic open before you try to get it closed down. I'd like to see a new business in town." Stew thought about how sincere she sounded. Maybe he had misjudged her. Maybe, just maybe, there was more to 'Miss Invisible' than he gave her credit for.

Of course, Buck did not appreciate the way this conversation was headed. No sir, not one bit. He had to put her in her place. "What you mean is, you'd like to see a new man in town."

Marcie, the ever-present tension reducer, came to her defense. "There goes your present from Santa. Miss Murphy is right. This town needs new blood if it's to survive."

Having now counted every towel and washcloth, twice in fact, Stew was beginning to feel like a peeping Tom and decided he should just go on back to his room and wait 'til someone called him to supper. He gently closed the hall closet door and had taken two steps back toward his room when Joey's words sent a chill up his spine. A chill that no amount of heat could thaw.

"Think how much it'll help Old Man Sloan to have a real doctor in town."

Marcie's response barely registered with Stew. "Joey, I have told you not to refer to him as Old Man Sloan. It's disrespectful."

"So is he!"

"He's not disrespectful, he's, he's..."

"Yes?"

"Lonely. He's lonely, that's all. Now, let's not ruin our supper with this kind of talk. Miss Murphy, would you like to see if Stew is ready for supper?"

As he heard Miss Murphy answer, "Right away", he forced himself to turn around and look as if he was already on his way to the living room. He had the forethought to reach over and open and close his bedroom door loudly before he entered Miss Murphy's line of vision. After what he had just heard, sounding casual would call on the best acting skills of his career. He spoke as soon as he saw Miss Murphy. "No need. My stomach told me it was almost suppertime. I'm looking forward to some of Marcie's famous fried chicken and apple pie."

Buck's response was predictable. "Well, it ain't the Colonels', but it'll fill the whole in your gut."

Marcie spoke good-naturedly. "I'll take that as a compliment."

"Take it any way you like. Just stating a fact."

In one fluid motion, Elizabeth entered the living room, exclaimed "Come and get it while the getting's good," and swept back through the swinging door to the dining room.

Joey seemed to speak for everyone as he jumped up from his desk. "Great! I'm starved!"

As they ambled toward the dining room, Marcie mentioned offhandedly to Stew, "I'm really impressed with all you've accomplished so far at the clinic. That place was a real eyesore, even before Doc Holland took it over as his vet clinic. It's one of the few buildings in town that survived the big fire. Personally, I think it would have been better had it burned."

Stew asked, "Was that the fire of 1912 or 1928?"

Buck was quick to impress Stew with his knowledge of local history. "It was the fire of 1912. That was the big one. My dad used to say that when the town burned the first time, it was God's way of telling us we had no business taking this land away from the Indians, and the few businesses that survived should have taken the hint and moved on, but of course no one listened to him. I'll say one thing for the stubborn cowboys around here, they have tenacity."

Stew looked Buck in the eye as he said, "Well, I don't know much about Ronan cowboys, but I sure could use a healthy dose of that tenacity myself. There's times when I wonder if all the work is worth it. Maybe I should just pack up and return to New York."

Joey's serious expression bore just a hint of a smile as he told Stew, "If you give up that easily, maybe you're right."

As Stew took his place in line behind Joey, he thought it was time to put the next part of step three in motion. He spoke as if a thought had just entered his mind. "Say, I was so tired when I came in this evening, that I didn't notice that mighty fine Christmas tree."

Marcie's response was both an apology and a hope. "Well, it doesn't look very Christmassy yet. Maybe after supper you can help us decorate it?"

"I'd love to, but I make it a habit to go to bed early on Saturday night so I can get up refreshed and ready for church on Sunday. I've been out of town the last several weekends on business trips, so this will be my first Sunday in church here."

Buck was quick with his snicker. "Church? There ain't no church in this town."

"What do you mean? I saw that little clapboard church when I first arrived. It's at the end of Main Street."

Murphy's voice was surprisingly sad as she spoke. "Doc, that church has been closed for years. Even the church mice don't live there anymore. There isn't a parson within fifty miles of here."

"But are there Christians in town?"

"Yes, at least I think so, but..."

"Then I'm going to church tomorrow. For now, let's get some of that chicken. Maybe after supper there will still be time to at least get started on that Christmas tree."

CHAPTER FOUR

Once Upon A Sunday

It had been a quiet Saturday night in Ronan. At least, a lot more quiet than his home in New York would have been. Funny, he thought, I've only been here a few weeks and I'm already beginning to lose the feeling that my real home is New York. No sirens, no cops. I could get used to this life. No, he realized, he had better not start thinking that way. It was too risky. He must always be on his toes. Always be aware that one wrong word and everyone would know the truth about Dr. Stewart Thomas. One wrong word and he would once again be on a bus headed for –where?

Having corralled his thoughts, he quietly stepped from his room into the kitchen hoping to get a cup of coffee before church. He was surprised to see everyone up and dressed in their Sunday best. Marcie was the first to greet him.

"Good mornin', Stew. We were wondering when you were going to get up. Breakfast is almost ready."

"Apparently New Yorkers sleep till noon," Buck interjected. "By then we've done a full day's work."

"Not on Sunday, I hope," laughed Stew. "Even God rested one day a week."

"God's not a cowboy," Buck drawled. Stew couldn't tell whether Buck was serious or teasing. Not knowing for sure how to respond, Stew decided it was best to change the subject.

"I'm surprised you're all up. Last night you were all trying to convince me not to go to church this morning, and now it looks like you're planning on going with me. What gives?"

"Easy," Buck answered. "If a man's gonna make a fool of himself, there oughta be someone around to appreciate it."

Miss Murphy stood to refill her coffee cup and leaned in to whisper in Stew's ear. "Don't mind him. I think he's as excited as you are about seeing that old church open again. Truth is, we would all like to see that church open. It's been too long since we've had anyone around here to remind us of God's Word. There used to be a strong Christian community here, but over time I think we've all drifted away. Not that we're all that bad, mind you. We're just not as close to God as we used to be."

"What could cause a whole town to drift away?" Stew asked. "That's not natural. An individual drifting away from God, now that I can understand. But a whole town? That doesn't make sense."

Marcie's answer brought Stew more questions. "About twenty years ago something happened in town. I don't know all the details, but what I do know is that it caused a church split. Well, split isn't exactly the right word. Truth is, the church just died and we never got around to burying it. We just closed it up and ignored it. For twenty years that building has stood as a reminder of something to all of us. Of what, I'm not sure."

Joey's mind was beginning to put some things together. "Twenty years ago? But Mom, that would be when..."

"Come on, Joey," she interrupted him. "We're going to be late."

———

Stew was both pleased and surprised at how many townspeople had shown up on such short notice. The only explanation he could come up with was that Marcie must have been on the phone late into the night 'calling in favors'. He didn't know the small church could hold so many people. Most, he thought, had probably come out of mere curiosity rather than a true spiritual hunger. No matter the reason, he rationalized, he was glad the church was full. Burl had even managed to clear the sidewalk of last week's accumulation of snow and had started the old church furnace. Surprisingly, it still worked.

Considering that he'd had such a short time to prepare his sermon, he was confident with his delivery. Although later, when asked individually, few of the townspeople could repeat his simple outline or even the title of his sermon, everyone seemed to have positive memories of the service, and that pleased him even more than whether or not anyone could remember his Scripture references. It appeared as everyone left the church that morning that Ronan was once again thinking in spiritual terms. And that was something he could work with.

Later, after a quick lunch at home, everyone went their separate ways for the afternoon, each with their own private agenda. After a short nap, Stew entered the living room to sit in front of the fire-place with his Bible and notebook. It looked to him as if he may be the new pastor in town, by default if nothing else, so he wanted to get a head start on next Sunday's sermon. If all worked out as scheduled, he would be ready to reveal his plans on the unsuspecting townspeople within the next two or three weeks. He just needed to lay a little more groundwork first.

He had been working for about an hour when he heard a small cough, and looked up to see Joey next to him holding what appeared to be a notebook identical to his own. Had Joey possibly seen Stew's notebook, and gone out and gotten the same one? Could Joey be admiring him, or was it possible that Joey already had an identical notebook, and this was nothing more than a coincidence? Joey seemed nervous. "Doc, have you got a minute?"

"I have all afternoon. What's on your mind?" Stew motioned for Joey to sit in the rocker next to him. Joey hesitated as he sat. He was clearly uncomfortable.

"Since everyone's gone for the day, I thought we might talk."

Stew set his Bible and notebook down on the end table next to his chair. "Sounds good to me. I was about half asleep sitting here. Where is everyone?"

"Mom and Grandma went to check on Old--on Mr. Sloan. He hasn't been to town for several weeks, and they were concerned about him. He had a bad fall last winter and he's had a difficult time ever since. He doesn't have any family, and it's hard for him to get around on his own anymore He's too stubborn to ask anyone for help."

"I understand." It was true. From his experience as a doctor and one-time preacher, Stew had worked with many elderly men and women who were too stubborn, or as they preferred to be known as, 'independent' for their own good. It was easy for Stew to picture Mr. Sloan as being too proud to accept, or even ask for help; no matter how much he may need it. The doctor in Stew was curious for more information on Mr. Sloan.

"Anyway," Joey's words brought Stew back to the moment. "Mom and Grandma went to check on him, and Miss Murphy and Buck went into town together on some secret mission."

"You mean 'together'? After last night, I figured Miss Murphy and Buck would be the last two people who would want to be seen together."

"That?" Joey laughed. "Believe me,

it's all talk. Buck just talks mean because he thinks that's what a cowboy is supposed to do. And Miss Murphy, I know she really likes him, she's just shy is all. I guess that's why they call her 'Miss' Murphy."

Stew thought on that for a moment before he responded. "You know, Joey, you're really observant. Someday that will help you become a great writer."

Joey couldn't hide the excitement in his voice. He didn't even try to. "Think so?"

Stew's smile said at least as much as his words. "I think so. And Joey, I'm sorry about what I said to you at the clinic. I didn't mean..."

"It's okay. I know what you meant. I figured it out after I cooled down. You were only trying to help."

"You really are observant."

"I try to be."

"Know what I've observed, Joey?"

"What?"

"That you're the only cowboy I know that doesn't have a cowboy hat. How 'bout we go downtown after the snow stops and pick you out a nice one? Every cowboy has to have a hat. Kind of like being a doctor without a stethoscope. My treat."

Joey stammered. "I-I-can't."

"Why? If it's about money, it's my treat. I want to do this."

Joey was almost whispering now, as if he was ashamed. "No, it's not about money. It's, well, have you heard Buck call me 'Greenhorn'?"

"Sure, but he's just teasing. What does that have to do with a cowboy hat?"

"It's a tradition around here," Joey explained simply. "He calls me 'Greenhorn' because he knows I don't like it, and because that's what I am. Around here you're called 'Greenhorn' until you do something that proves you're a real cowboy. That's when you get your first hat. You can't buy it yourself, someone else has to get it for you or it doesn't count. It's like a badge of honor or a rite of passage. Once you have proven to someone that you're a real cowboy, then you get your first hat. To Buck, I will always be a 'Greenhorn'. Maybe he's right. He's always telling me I don't know anything about life. That I can't become a real writer because I haven't had any real experiences yet."

Stew dismissed Joey's last statement with a wave of his hand. "That's nonsense. You've had plenty of experiences to write about."

"Like what?" Joey's question was sincere.

"Like Thunder."

"That's not experience. That's humiliation."

"And what did you learn from your humiliation?" Stew asked.

Joey couldn't help but laugh. "That pride goeth before a fall, but much faster afterwards."

"Then write that," Stew admonished.

"Why? No one wants to read about falling off a horse."

"Joey, have you ever ridden a subway?"

"Of course not. I've never even seen one, except on television."

"That's my point. The people in New York ride subways everywhere without thinking anything of it. But very few New Yorkers have had the opportunity to get bucked off a horse. The life of a Montana cowboy would be an exciting adventure for them."

"I guess so." Joey didn't sound very sure.

Stew put his hand on Joey's shoulder. At that moment he truly wished Joey was his son. He wanted to share with Joey all the experiences he had not been able to share with his own father. "Joey, don't write about experiences you're still waiting for. Write what you already know about."

"Doc, I'm only a Montana cowboy."

"You're not 'only a Montana cowboy'. You *are* a Montana cowboy. And always remember, Joey, you can take the cowboy out of Montana but you can't take Montana out of the cowboy. So don't try."

"Thanks for the advice, Doc. I think you understand me better than anyone else does, except maybe Mom. But she's 'Mom' so she doesn't count. Don't tell her I said that."

Stew's voice was sincere. "Joey, I'd like to read some of your writing sometime. If you don't mind."

"I appreciate that, Doc, but no one's ever read my work. Not even Mom. I'm not ready for that yet. And speaking of work, I need to go brush down Thunder before I put him in for the night."

"Need some help?" Stew offered.

"Nah. I think he's beginning to like me." He turned to leave before completing his thought. "See you at supper."

"Sure." Stew remembered something as Joey started for the door. "Uh, Joey, when you came in you said you wanted to talk, but I've done most of the talking. Was there something else on your mind?"

With his hand on the doorknob, Joey turned to face him. "I almost forgot. I wanted to thank you for preaching this morning. It did this town a lot of good to hear a sermon again."

"Thanks, but I'm not really a preacher. I tried that once for a while, but--well, lets just say I have a more effective ministry as a doctor than as a pastor. This way I can still help people without having to--say, didn't you have to brush down Thunder?"

"Right. See you at supper." Once more Joey started to leave, paused, and turned back to face Stew. "Oh, Doc, I know I said I'm not ready for anyone to read my work yet, but I've got some things here from other writers. I've never shown them to anyone before, but, well, I'd like to show them to you--if you don't mind."

"I'd like that very much." Stew was surprised at how much he meant the words. "Do you have a favorite?"

"Well, I like this one," Joey said as he thumbed through the pages of his notebook. "It's a cowboy prayer. I found it in a magazine. I don't understand all of what it says, but I think I understand all of what it feels."

"Let's hear it." Stew sat as if he were preparing to hear a great orator.

"A Cowboy's Christmas Prayer," Joey began in his most professional voice. "By S. Barker."

'I ain't much good at prayin', Lord,

And You may not know me. For I ain't
much seen in churches,
Where they preach Thy Holy Word.
But You may have seen me, Lord,
Out here on the lonely plains.
A-lookin' after cattle, and feelin' thankful
when it rains.
Admirin' Thy great handiwork,
The miracle of the grass-
Aware of Thy kind Spirit,
In the way it comes to pass-
That hired help on horseback,
And the cattle that we tend,
Can look up at the stars at night,
And know we've got a Friend.
So here's Ol' Christmas comin' on,
Reminding us again
Of Him whose coming brought good will
Into the hearts of men.
A cowboy ain't no preacher, Lord,
But if You'll hear my prayer-
I'll ask as good as we have got-
For all men everywhere.
Don't let no hearts be bitter, Lord.
Don't let no child be cold.
Make easy the bed for them that's sick,
And them that's weak and old.
Let kindness bless the trail we ride,
No matter what we're after.
And sorta keep us on Your side,
In tears as well as laughter.
I've seen old cows a-starvin'-

It ain't no happy sight.
Please don't leave no one hungry,
Lord,
On Thy good Christmas Night.
No man, no child, no woman,
And no critter on four feet.
I'll do my doggone best to help You
Find them chuck to eat.
I'm just a sinful cowpoke, Lord,
But still I hope You'll ketch a word
Or two of what I'm sayin'.
We speak of Merry Christmas, Lord,
But I reckon You'll agree-
There ain't no Merry Christmas,
For nobody that ain't free!
So one more thing I ask of You, Lord,
Just help us what You can
To save some seeds of freedom-for the
future sons of man.'"

Stew's response was soft and thoughtful. "I'm with you, Joey. I think I understand how he feels. And you know what? I'll just bet whoever wrote that probably never rode a subway either."

"Think so?"

"Think so."

"Thanks, Doc. Well, Thunder's waitin'. See you at supper."

Stew watched Joey as he carefully placed his journal on the table and walked out the door, closing it behind him. Stew picked up his own Bible and notebook and started for the kitchen when he remembered Joey's journal and picked it up to return to his own bedroom. It was then that he heard the sounds of a wild horse. Joey's own screams were lost under the sound of his own voice as it caught in his throat. He screamed the only word he knew to scream. There was no one else around to hear him scream "Joey!"

———————

Two hours later, everyone had returned from their various wanderings around town and had gotten over their initial shock and concern over seeing Joey lying on the couch with his boot off and his foot propped up on several pillows. Stew's words were meant to comfort Marcie as much as Joey, maybe even more so. "It's going to be pretty sore for awhile, and it'll be a few weeks before Ol' Thunder bucks you off again, but..."

"Doc, I'm never getting near that horse again!"

Marcie sounded just like a mother. "Sure you will. You know what they say about falling off a bicycle."

"Mom, Thunder ain't no bicycle. I'm telling you I'm not ever..."

Stew knew it was time to sound like a doctor. "Well, not for a couple weeks, anyway. Marcie, it looks like you were right about Joey and Thunder keeping me in business. Since our distraction with our little Cowboy..."

"Greenhorn is more like it," Buck interrupted.

Stew ignored Buck as if he had not heard him. "Since Joey gave us a fright you haven't had a chance to tell us about your visit with, Mr. Sloan, is it?"

Marcie adjusted Joey's pillows as she spoke. "Mom and I didn't get to see him. That blizzard's coming in pretty fast. We saw Renae Anderson at the post office in town, and she said she would check on him for us. He doesn't live too far from her and she checks on him from time to time. She was concerned that we might not make it back before the blizzard hit full force. I offered to send Buck up to check on him..."

"I don't remember volunteering."

Marcie followed Stew's lead in ignoring Buck. "...But she reminded me that he had never been to Mr. Sloan's place and would never find it in the blizzard."

Elizabeth entered the room with a smile and a pie plate, walking directly to her grandson. "Here, Joey, I had one piece of apple pie left."

Joey did not look up. "Thanks, but I'm not hungry."

Elizabeth's tone matched her smile. "An apple a day keeps the--Oh, sorry, Doc."

Stew's laughter eased her embarrassment. "You're right. That apple pie is better medicine than anything I can give him right now."

"I'll just set it down here," Elizabeth said as she set the pie plate on the end table. She turned to Joey. "You can eat it when you're hungry." Having made certain that Joey was comfortable, Elizabeth turned her attention to Stew. "Say, Stew, I've been thinking about your sermon this morning. Especially about where you said that telling the truth frees the soul from bondage. What did you mean?"

Stew reached for his Bible where he had laid it down earlier and thumbed through the well-worn pages. "Let's see here. I think I can remember the Bible references I used. Here it is. Proverbs 12:19 says 'The lip of truth shall be established for ever: but a lying tongue is but for a moment.' And Zechariah 8:16 says: 'These are the things that ye shall do; Speak ye every man truth to his neighbor; execute the judgment of truth and peace in your gates.' To me, this means that when we lie, we bind ourselves to the bondage of living that lie. But when we are willing to forsake that lie and live according to the truth, we free ourselves from that bondage. If you always tell the truth, you don't have to remember what you said."

"I understand that part," Miss Murphy joined the conversation. "But what I don't understand is what you meant by 'presenting yourselves as a living sacrifice to God.'"

It was Buck's turn to join the conversation. "He meant 'if it's fun, don't do it.'"

"Not exactly, Buck," Stew answered patiently as he searched for another scripture. "The verse is Romans 12:1, and if you read the context of the rest of the chapter you'll see that the emphasis isn't on what we don't do, but what we do for God and others. Here, let me get my notes and I'll show you. My note journal should be around here somewhere. I was reading it just before Joey got hurt."

Everyone started to look for the journal, but it was Miss Murphy who found it. "Is that it there on the table?"

"Thanks," Stew said as he picked up the journal and read a few lines silently before he realized it was not his notebook, but Joey's. He set it back down on the table as he picked up the notebook that had been lying underneath it. He thumbed through his journal until he found what he was looking for. "Here it is. Romans 12." The ring of the phone stopped him as Marcie answered it.

"Hello. Stoneheart Inn."

"Marcie? This is Renae Anderson." Stew could hear the fear and concern in her voice. "You've got to get me Doctor Thomas. It's an emergency."

Marcie handed Stew the phone. "Doctor Thomas, you gotta hurry! It's Mr. Sloan." Stew's body burned and froze at the same time. "What is it?"

"I think he's had a stroke! Hurry!"

The first rule of any emergency is to remain calm, he told himself. "Wait! What happened?"

"No time to explain! Hurry!"

Stew forced himself to sound calm, as much for himself as for Renae Anderson on the other end of the phone line. "Look, I've got to know what happened to know how to help." He could tell that his voice was helping her to calm down. At least she was breathing easier.

"With the blizzard on its way, I wanted to get some extra supplies to Mr. Sloan before he got snowed in."

Marcie, hearing Renae's end of the conversation, tried to explain to Stew. "Renae is the lady I told you about. She is Mr. Sloan's closest neighbor, and has tried to keep an eye on him since his accident last year."

"Anyway," Renae continued, "I put some supplies in a couple boxes in the back of my truck. I knew with the heavy snow coming that my car would never make it up the mountain, and I wasn't even sure about the truck, but it made it. I knocked on the door, but he didn't answer. I knew he had to be there--he hasn't left that place since his accident. No matter how hard I knocked, he wouldn't answer, and I got scared so I kicked the door in. That's when I saw him lying on the floor. He was breathing heavy and his eyes were out of focus. He couldn't talk. He was just mumbling something over and over. I couldn't tell what it was. I didn't know what I could do, so I just put a blanket on him and got back home as fast as I could. I knew I had to call you, and Mr. Sloan doesn't have a phone. Please, Doctor, you've got to help him."

Stew's mind was reeling. There were so many things to consider. "All right. I'll get to the clinic and get my bag. Then..."

"No good. You may still make it to the clinic by truck, but there's no way in this snow that you'll make it back up the mountain--even in a four-wheel drive. I barely made it back to my place, and I'm his closest neighbor. You'll never find the road."

Marcie was frantic and bordering on panic as she listened to the conversation. "But we've got to do something! We can't just leave him there!"

Stew had to get control of the situation. And that meant keeping everyone calm. "Renae, I don't know how yet, but we'll get there as soon as possible. I'll make sure the phone line stays open in case you need to call or I need more information. For now, don't worry. I'll keep you posted. I'll do the doctoring, you just pray." As he hung up he turned to Marcie and continued, without stopping for a breath. "Marcie, you get a spare bed fixed up. We'll need lots of extra bedding too." He now gave orders as if he was in surgery. "Buck, you can still make it from here to the clinic and back before the snow gets too deep, if you hurry. My bag is in my office, bring that. There's a key in my top center desk drawer for the medicine cabinet behind the desk. There's no time for you to figure out the right medicines to bring. There are boxes in the front room where I've been unpacking things. Fill one of them with every medicine I've got. Bring that and..."

"Doc, I don't think that's the best..."

"Right now I don't care what you

think. I'm the doctor. Just go. Take Miss Murphy with you. She can help load the medicine." Buck just stood there, as if he had to think this through.

Stew reached for their coats on the rack next to the front door and threw them in their direction as he spoke. "Go!"

Buck and Miss Murphy pulled on coats as they closed the door behind them. Stew turned his attention to Elizabeth. "Elizabeth, get the biggest coffee pot you have. This is going to be a long night. We're also going to need sandwiches. And broth for William. We don't know for sure what happened to him or how long it's been since he's eaten. If I don't have to do any surgery, then I may need to try and get some nourishment in him."

Joey jumped into the excitement. "What can I do? There's got to be something that I can..."

"I hate to say this, Joey, but you're going to have to get Mr. Sloan yourself."

"I can't! I can't even walk!"

Putting his hand on Joey's shoulder, Stew became both friend and doctor. Maybe even a surrogate father. "Joey, I'm counting on you. We can't get to Mr. Sloan by truck. You're going to have to take Thunder. It's the only way to get up that mountain."

Joey was shaking with fear. "There's no way that I can..."

"It's the only way. Joey, you have to do this. There is no one else to send. Buck has never been to Mr. Sloan's cabin. He would never find it in the snow. And I've never been on a horse before in my life, so..."

Joey's eyes were pleading. "But you're a stallion trainer. I know that..."

"I'm a what?"

"Mom explained the ST tattoo to me. I know it stands for stallion trainer."

Stew put pressure on his shoulder and spoke firmly. "Joey, this is no time to talk about old tattoos. I'll explain later. Look, I know you're hurt and you're scared, but you can do this. I'll hook up Thunder to the sled out behind the barn. When you get to the cabin, make sure Mr. Sloan is as comfortable as possible. Then grab all the medicines you can find anywhere in the house. Check his night stand, medicine cabinet, kitchen counter, wherever he might have some pills. As soon as you have done that, carefully put Mr. Sloan on the sled. We don't know if he has any internal injuries, and he can't tell you if he does. Wrap him in as many blankets as you can find, then tie him down carefully in the sled and get him back here as quickly as you can."

Joey was almost in tears. "Doc, I can't even walk."

Stew had to admit that Joey was right. Still, there was no other choice. "Come on, Greenhorn, it's time you learned to just cowboy up and do it. Here, I'll help you with your boot." Stew knew that he had to distract Joey from thinking of himself. It only took one yell of pain from Joey for Stew to realize that he would never get Joey's cowboy boot back on his injured foot. Thinking fast, Stew unlaced his own work boot and, placing two small sticks from near the fireplace around Joey's leg, he wrapped them tightly with the shoelace. He then handed Joey a fireplace poker to use as a cane, and helped him to stand. With one arm around Joey's waist for support, he reached for their coats from the rack as he yelled, "Let's go!"

Joey winced in pain as he spoke. "Doc, you called Mr. Sloan 'William'. How did you know that was his name?"

Stew tried to quickly think of an answer as he watched Marcie enter the room. "You must have heard me wrong."

"I didn't hear you wrong."

"I must have heard you or Marcie call him that."

"Doc, we have never called him William. Now, how did you know that was his name?"

As Marcie came to Stew's rescue, Stew knew he would have some explaining to do. Some serious explaining. "Renae must have called him that on the phone."

"Mom, you know that..."

As Stew escorted Joey out the door, he knew that his life was about to change. He remembered a verse from the book of Job. Something about 'the thing that I greatly feared has come upon me.' As a doctor in surgery, he had been trained to think on his feet in any emergency situation. But no amount of quick thinking would help him now. "Let's just say that Ronan is a town of secrets, and leave it at that." As he turned to Marcie, he was certain that his life as he had planned it had just come to a crashing end. He could not bring himself to look at her as he spoke. "You and I need to talk as soon as I get Joey and Old Thunder taken care of. Come on, Joey, let's go." As he closed the door behind him, he closed the last chapter of his life as Doctor Stewart Thomas.

What is this strange power that Doc has over me? Joey wondered, as he clung to

Thunder's reins for dear life. I barely know the man, and yet. And yet. Those two words seemed to sum up his entire life.

Joey had always prided himself on not needing a father figure. And yet. He wasn't sure just exactly how or when it had happened. Later he would remember it as the time in Doc Stewart's clinic when Doc had first acknowledged that Joey's thoughts and dreams of being a writer were valid.

But now--now he must not think of these things. For now he had to concentrate on one thing--getting to Sloan's cabin. He had already gotten lost once trying to find the cabin. He could not afford to get lost a second time. Not in this blizzard.

The snow was now up to Thunder's underside, making it nearly impossible for him to trudge up the mountain. He wasn't sure how far he had come. Five miles? Seven? It couldn't be much further. The last time he had been to Sloan's cabin was right after Sloan's accident last year. But now is not the time to think of the past, he reminded himself. Concentrate, Joey, Sloan's cabin can't be much further.

With his head bent down against the wind and with the snow in his face, it was hard to concentrate on the road ahead of him. Well, actually, it was no longer a road. It had been reduced to a mere trail several miles back. Now it wasn't even much of a trail. Wait, he thought. This doesn't seem right. I know that Sloan's cabin is close by, but I don't remember this trail. Wishing he had a cowboy hat to block the wind, he realized there was nothing he could do at this point except turn back and try to find where he had gotten off the main road. It couldn't be far. Could it?

As he slowly turned Thunder to head back in the direction he had just come from, he noticed that Thunder's previous trail was almost completely buried in new snow. Joey's hands and feet were numb to the point he knew he was close to frostbite. He also knew he couldn't last much longer in this blizzard. He was starting to get sleepy. That was a bad sign. If he didn't reach Sloan's cabin in the next twenty minutes, he knew he would die, and his body might not be found until the spring thaw. That thought drove him on.

Just ahead, what's that? A light? Yes! Renae must have left a light on in Sloan's cabin. He knew he could now make it to the cabin, but could he make it back home? One step at a time, Joey, he reminded himself. One step at a time.

Approaching the cabin, he did not want to frighten the old man with his sudden appearance, so he spoke, slowly and loudly, to Thunder as he dismounted. "Whoa, there, boy. We're here. We made it. We're just going to check on Mr. Sloan and then get you back to your nice warm barn. All right? Good boy, Thunder." As he finished dismounting, he realized that his injured foot did not hurt. A benefit of the cold, he reminded himself. The real pain would come later.

The tracks from Renae's truck had long since been buried, but he could see where she had kicked in the front door. Though she had attempted to close the door, the latch had been broken and the door would not close tight. Fresh snow on the floor sparkled and glistened in the light from the single lamp in the room.

As Joey entered the cabin, his eyes darting quickly from one end of the small room to the other, he saw Sloan lying on the floor, still covered with the blanket Renae had put over him. Sloan looked like he was--Joey would not allow himself to complete the thought. Pulling off his gloves with his teeth, Joey tried to feel for Mr. Sloan's pulse, but his own hands were too numb to feel anything.

Knowing he had little time to work-- and not knowing if Mr. Sloan was even alive, he forced himself to remember Doc's instructions. As he worked, he continued speaking, partly to ease Sloan's fears, but mostly to ease his own. Where did Doc say to look for medicines? He tried to clear his mind. Night stand. Medicine cabinet. Kitchen counter. Got it. Putting the medicines in his saddlebag, he again turned his complete attention to Sloan.

Taking all of the bedding off the only bed in the cabin, he wrapped the blankets around Sloan as tight as possible. He then brought in the sled, barely getting it in the narrow front door. He had no idea whether or not Sloan could hear him, but he continued speaking out loud while working both inside and outside the house.

Having wrapped Sloan tightly in the blankets, he still had to find a way to effectively, and safely, tie him to the sled. He reprimanded himself harshly for failing to think to bring a rope. He was a Greenhorn, indeed. What could he do? Wait, he had an idea. What if--it just might work. Quickly taking his pocketknife from his pants pocket he stepped out the back door. Fastened to the back wall of the house was the clothesline, stretching from the house to the barn. Cutting off twenty feet of line, he used it to wrap around Sloan and the sled, mummy style.

Joey had never been a boy scout, but he figured his knots would hold, at least until he made it home.

Joey would later remember very little of the ride back home. Thunder would make it back to the barn on willpower and instinct alone. With gravity's help down the mountain, mixed with constant prayer and periodic stops to check on Sloan, Joey knew he would make it home safely. That thought did nothing to warm his hands and feet, but it did warm his heart.

CHAPTER FIVE

The Sloan Connection

Over the next three hours Elizabeth was kept busy in the kitchen, making sandwiches and keeping the coffee pot full. Buck and Miss Murphy had barely made it to town and back before the radio announced that the state patrol had closed off all roads between St. Ignatius and Polson, meaning there would be no travel anywhere near Ronan. Buck and Miss Murphy were trying to stay occupied with a game of checkers, but neither of them was able to concentrate. Marcie was pacing back and forth from the kitchen to the living room, trying hard to be helpful and even harder not to worry about Joey somewhere out in that blizzard. She wasn't succeeding. And Stew was simply trying to hold everything together, knowing all the while that regardless of what happened here tonight, he would be on the first bus out of Ronan when the roads cleared. He didn't know where he would go, and right now he didn't care. For now his only concern was to get himself, and everyone else at the Stoneheart Inn, through both the blizzard that raged outside and the blizzard that raged inside.

Elizabeth entered from the kitchen, carrying a plate of sandwiches to put next to the plate of sandwiches that no one had touched. "Would anyone like any more...?"

"No more food!" barked Buck. "Food is not the answer to everything!"

"I'm sorry. I was only trying to help." One more word and Elizabeth would have started crying.

Murphy stepped in. "Thank you, Elizabeth. We know you just want to help. He didn't mean it."

Buck did not look up as he spoke. "I can speak for myself." He then surprised everyone by softly adding, "I'm sorry. We're all just a little tense. The waiting's the hardest part."

Marcie quickly stepped to the window and pulled back the curtain, even though it was dark outside. "I heard something outside. Are they here yet?"

Stew wanted to offer comfort, but

there wasn't much he could say. "It's just the wind. Don't worry. They'll be here any minute."

"How can you say 'Don't worry'? That's not your son out there in the blizzard. How could you send him out there like that? You don't even know if he made it to Mr. Sloan's cabin. For all you know he could be--he could be..." she turned her face away from them all to cry.

Stew could not wait any longer. The issues had to be dealt with. Now. He turned to face everyone, knowing that they would not be returning the gaze. "Everyone, why don't you all go make sure everything is set up in the spare room. Marcie and I need to talk."

As soon as everyone had left the room, Marcie turned to face him. Her face was streaked with tears. For Joey or for him he could not tell. "I didn't mean that. I'm just scared. I know you did what you thought was best. It's just that..." her voice trailed off.

He could no longer avoid the question he already knew the answer to. "You know who I am, don't you?"

Her answer was not the one he had expected. "Or who you're not. You're not Stew Thomas."

"How did you find out?"

"It wasn't hard. When you run a boarding house you meet a lot of friendly people who like to talk. Especially the old timers."

"Do the others know?"

"I doubt it. No one has said anything." She forced a small smile. "Don't flatter yourself, you're not the only topic of conversation around here."

Stew was confused about something. Several things, really. "Why did you tell Joey that my mark stood for 'stallion trainer'?"

"It's all I could think of at the moment. I may be a good cook, but I've never claimed to be very creative."

Stew was ashamed. More ashamed than he had ever been in his life. "So you know my name isn't Stew Thomas. Are you going to tell the others about me?"

Marcie pondered her answer thoughtfully. The truth was, she had already made up her mind about what she was going to do. But there was no reason for her to let Stew know that. "Not unless you give me a reason to tell them. As you said earlier, we all have our secrets." *And that includes me,* Marcie thought.

"How long have you known?"

"Since we met. I saw your mark when you put your watch on in the clinic."

"You still haven't told me why the

story about my being a stallion trainer."

Marcie weighed her words carefully. "Like I said, it's all I could think of at the time. I didn't know whether or not Joey had seen the mark and I needed to be prepared if he asked me about it. It wasn't hard to figure out that you made up the name Stew Thomas as a cover for the mark--something you could explain to New Yorkers and strangers on the street when they asked about it. But I knew that if Joey accidentally mentioned it to the wrong people around here, it could mean trouble for you. Trouble you might not be able to explain away very easily. I had to come up with something just in case."

Stew did not have to pretend the sincerity in his voice. "I appreciate that. But what can I do now? I've blown my own cover. I told Joey that I've never been on a horse, so how could I be a stallion trainer?"

"Is this where I say 'Physician, heal thyself'? You could start by telling the truth. I've heard it's good at freeing the soul from bondage. A wise man once said that if you always tell the truth, you don't have to remember what you said. Whatever there is I don't know about you, I still believe what you told me when we met. That you want to be a healer of broken bones and broken hearts. And I still believe that God has called you here as a healer. Even if right now you may not believe it yourself."

"Caught again. But that's different. I didn't mean to hurt anyone. I only meant to..." The sound of Joey and Thunder stopped all conversation.

Marcie ran toward the front door. All thoughts of Stew were forced out of her mind immediately. Only one thing was important now. "Joey! He's back!"

Stew caught her just before she reached the door. He turned her quickly with his strong arm on her shoulder. He forced her to face him as he spoke. His voice was firm but quiet, to make sure no one else heard him. "I need to explain about..."

She squirmed out of his hold. Her voice was equally soft. And equally firm. "We will finish this later. Don't worry. You aren't the only one in Ronan that can keep a secret. Right now you are Doctor Stewart Thomas, and you are needed. There is a boy out there in the snow who believes you are a God-send, and for the first time in his life he has a father figure, and..."

"I did not ask to be a father figure."

"Right now I am not concerned with what you want. I won't let anyone take that away from him. Not even you. You will think up something to tell him, and whether I like it or not I'll go along with whatever you say. I'll keep your secret, at least for now. Besides, I'm not the one you need to explain things to. You had better think fast, Doc, because everyone here is about to get the shock of their lives and I'm not sure we're ready for it."

PART TWO

CHAPTER SIX

The Confrontation

Everyone had gone out to help Joey and Mr. Sloan. Surprisingly, it was Buck who reached his arm around Joey to help him from Thunder and into the house. Stew and Marcie had carried in the sled, afraid to move Mr. Sloan until they knew more about the extent of his condition. Mr. Sloan lay on the sled in front of the fireplace, staring uncomprehendingly as Stew labored over him, replacing the wet blankets with dry ones that Elizabeth and Miss Murphy brought in. The fire was roaring and comfortable.

Joey's first words were as much a prayer as a declaration. "Thank God we made it." Stew's response was almost a mumble. "Yes, Thank God."

Joey felt a need to talk, as if his words helped him think through the events of the last few hours. "We weren't sure we would make it. I got lost twice, just getting to the cabin."

Marcie handed Joey a hot cup of coffee as she pulled the blanket up tighter around his shoulders. She knew she was mothering him, but she didn't care. Neither did he. She tried to hold in all of her conflicting emotions as she spoke. "Well, you made it, and you're safe now. That's all that matters."

Joey's hands were still shaking as he sipped the strong coffee. "I stopped as often as I could to get the snow off him. I didn't want him to freeze on top of everything else."

Stew's words and tone of voice were as much for Marcie as for Joey. "You did good. I'm proud of you."

Buck surprised everyone, but no one wanted it to show. He cleared his throat as he spoke, attempting to sound offhanded. "So am I, Cowboy. Let Doc take over now. Here, let me help you with that boot." As Buck continued to speak, he worked on getting Joey's 'boot' off. Joey was too dumbfounded to respond. "That foot must be hurtin' somethin' fierce. And you gotta be as frozen as Mr. Sloan."

Joey found his voice. "Surprising as

this is, I'm not. I was so cold and hurtin' so bad I didn't think I'd make it, but once I got so busy helping him I forgot about myself. I barely hurt at all now. And I didn't have time to think how scared I was of Thunder. Once he saw how determined I was, he stopped fighting me."

Only low guttural sounds came from Mr. Sloan as Stew continued to check him over. It was obvious that he was scared and wanted to speak, but could not make himself understood. It seemed to Marcie that Stew was as concerned with Mr. Sloan's not speaking as he was his overall condition. Elizabeth came in with a plate of sandwiches and an announcement. She set the food on the coffee table as she spoke to Stew. "Mr. Sloan's room is all set up. What else can we do?"

Stew continued to work as he answered her. He did not look at anyone besides Mr. Sloan as he spoke. "For the moment, I want to keep him here by the fire until he's warm clear through. Buck, I need you to bring in some of those shop lights from the barn. Hook them up on anything you can find in Mr. Sloan's room, so I'll have operating lights if necessary. Miss Murphy, take all the medicine bottles that Joey brought and put them on the left hand side of Mr. Sloan's dresser. Put them in order of dosage, beginning with what he probably took this morning. Then make me a chart of all the medicines and tack it on the wall. I need to know the names of every medicine, the dosage, and when taken. Next to those medicines, line up all the medicines that you and Buck brought back from the clinic, in alphabetical order. I also need the first aid kit with my thermometer, stethoscope, and blood pressure cuff left out on the top of the dresser. Joey, you're going to be my medical assistant--just in case. But first, I need you to get a notebook and write down some observations for me. Write down anything you observed in Mr. Sloan's cabin that might be helpful--food left out on the counter, where and how it looked like he fell, anything he may have been holding when you found him. That kind of thing. Then write down any observations about his appearance or behavior. How he looked, how he felt to the touch, what he may have tried to say. Got it?"

Joey answered a quick "Yes, sir" as he walked away to find a notebook.

Stew continued giving directions. "Marcie, I need two large bowls of hot water and several towels. One bowl will be to use for Mr. Sloan. The other will be used for disinfecting and sanitizing his room. I need that small cart from the kitchen--the one with wheels--and I need you to put on it every cleaning supply you have. Elizabeth, we're going to need that broth for Mr. Sloan, but not too hot. We also need lots of coffee, sandwiches, and fruit. We all have to take shifts watching Mr. Sloan through the night and the food will keep us going. Buck said that food wasn't the answer to everything, but at least for tonight, it's the answer for a lot of things. Okay, everyone, you have your duties. Let's get this clinic open for business. I'll take the first watch. If all goes well, then Buck, I'll have you help me move Mr. Sloan into his room in about two hours. Then you and Miss Murphy can take the next watch. You can keep each other company. That'll make the night go easier. For now, everyone try and get a little rest. I'll call if I need you."

Stew acknowledged everyone's comments of 'Just call if you need me' and waited patiently until everyone had left the room before he bent down and whispered to Mr. Sloan in a voice he had not used in twenty years. "Okay, Mr. Sloan, you and I need a little talk." He watched the fear in Mr. Sloan's eyes and knew that he was understood. "I'll talk, you just listen." Mr. Sloan tried to scream, but nothing came out of his mouth except bubbles. Stew put his index finger on Sloan's mouth. "Sh! We don't want the others coming back in here, now do we? At least not yet. You'll be able to talk again soon, but for now it's best you keep quiet. It's not like you have a choice though, is it? I know you've had quite a shock--and I don't mean your stroke. First, you need to know you're going to be fine. Whatever else I am, I'm a good doctor. It'll take awhile, but you'll be fine. I don't want you worrying about that. Now, about what's really on your mind. I know you didn't expect to see me again, and frankly I didn't expect to ever see you again, at least not like this. I don't have time to tell you all about it now. I don't know when someone might walk in on us. But trust me--I know, coming from me that doesn't mean much, but trust me anyway. I'm not here to hurt you. I know you're ashamed of me, but that's why I came back. I have to..." He heard someone in the next room as Joey walked through the dining room and into the living room. Again, he put his finger on Mr. Sloan's lips and whispered very softly, "Hush up, old man, if you know what's best for you." He looked up to see Joey standing next to him. "I'm sorry to disturb you. I found a notebook but I needed a pen from my desk."

"...and I have to get a cup of coffee. It's going to be a long night."

———————

Mr. Sloan had been sleeping fitfully for a couple hours in front of the fire while Stew dozed on and off in the arm chair next to the Christmas tree. Stew roused when he heard steps in the kitchen. He stiffly rose, stretched, and checked on Mr. Sloan one more time, deciding that it was probably safe to move him into his own room, just as Marcie walked through the kitchen door into the living room. They glanced at each other knowingly, each wanting to speak volumes but neither saying a word. Finally, embarrassed, Stew asked, "Something on your mind?"

"No. Yes. Let's talk."

"Here?"

"No. I think the snow's stopped. Let's step out on the porch. I don't want anyone to hear us."

"Good idea." Stew wordlessly grabbed their coats from the rack next to the front door. He first put on his own coat, helped Marcie into hers, and they stepped out on to the porch, quietly closing the door behind them.

The blizzard had indeed stopped. The

thick blanket of white brought with it a hushed, haunting calm. A calm neither of them felt. For a long moment each of them was silent, buried under their own burdens. As he leaned against the corner porch rail, Stew was the first to speak. "So, what now?"

"I don't know." Again, silence permeated the night.

"Marcie, you're the one that said you had something on your mind. What are you thinking about?"

"Nothing. Everything. What about you?"

"The same."

"Well, Stew, have you come up with any answers?"

"I'm not even sure I know what the questions are any more. This changes everything."

"This?"

"Mr. Sloan. Joey. You and me."

"There is no 'you and me'."

"You know what I mean."

"No, Stew, I don't. But I need to. I want to."

Suddenly Stew had a burning desire to tell her everything. Who he really was, why he had come to Ronan. Everything his heart had ever felt. But he only said, "Okay. Where do you want me to start?"

"How about with who you really are.

Why you are here?"

"I can only tell you that I can't tell you."

"'Can't' or 'Won't'?"

"Does it really matter?"

For the first time in years, she intentionally lied. "I suppose not. But tell me this: why Ronan? It's as far from everything in New York as possible."

"That's the idea. I needed a change, simple as that."

"Are you in trouble with the law? Or a woman?" She wasn't sure she wanted to hear his answer.

"No, at least not the way you're thinking. There was a woman once, a long time ago." As he turned away to look at nothing in particular he suddenly realized for the first time that he could have feelings--strong feelings--for Marcie. If things were different, he reminded himself. He adjusted the Welcome Friends doormat with his boot as he finished his thought. "We met in Bib- we met in college. We dated seriously for a couple years and planned to get married right after I completed my internship. But by the time my internship was over, we both realized that marriage would be a mistake. I had a mistress. That's what she called it, anyway. She said I could never love or be committed to anyone as much as I was to my work. When I honestly thought about it, I realized that she was right. After we broke off our engagement I never dated again. I lost myself in my work."

"Are you still lost?"

"I don't know if I'm still lost or not, but I'm willing to look at a map."

"Where is it you want to go?"

"Somewhere that-- nowhere in particular."

"Ronan is about as 'nowhere in particular' as you can get."

"Then I guess I must be home." He wasn't sure, but he thought he saw hurt, or maybe compassion, in her eyes. "Marcie, I know you want, you deserve, some answers from me. You must be confused by all this. I know I am. But I can't give you those answers, at least not yet anyway. Maybe someday."

"'Somedays' never come." Until this moment, Marcie had convinced herself that she needed answers for Joey's sake, so Joey would not be hurt. But now, looking into Stew's eyes, she knew that wasn't true. At least not completely true. She needed answers for her own sake. As she confronted Stew Thomas, she also confronted her own memories, her own past. Looking at him face to face, she spoke with more boldness than she felt.

"Stew Thomas--and I know that is not your real name--I don't know why you are here, and I may never know. I can live with that. Whatever you are hiding from, I don't care. But I do care about everyone inside this house and I will not let you hurt them--any of them." She paused just long enough to let this sink in.

"As I see it, this is where we stand: I do believe you are a doctor, I've seen your work. And I believe that you came from New York. Beyond those two things I question everything about you. What you are hiding from concerns me, but it does not frighten me. Some part of you down deep inside is living a lie, and eventually that lie will be exposed. When that happens, and mark my words, it will happen, I will be here to help you in any way I can. But know this, and know it well--if necessary, I am capable of doing my own investigation. And if I ever have any reason to think that your lie will hurt someone I care for, then I will not hesitate to expose you. You are welcome to stay here as long as you want or need to; just keep your suitcase handy. Do we have an understanding?"

"Yes sir, Ma'am, we have an understanding. But as long as we are putting our cards on the table, let me ask you a question."

"Go on."

"If, as you believe, I am not Stew Thomas, why are you so willing to accept my secret?"

"Everyone has secrets, Stew."

"Even you?"

"Even me."

"I find that hard to believe. I don't think you're capable of lying to anyone."

"There is more than one kind of lie, Stew. There's the obvious, blatant lie. There's the lie when someone asks what you think of their hairdo and you tell them it looks great even though you hate it. Then there's the lie when you don't tell all that you know. It isn't that you purposely lie; you simply keep back information, convincing yourself that it's the only way to prevent hurting someone."

"Is that what you have done?"

"It's cold out here. I think it's time to go back inside."

My story? I never thought of it in those terms before, she realized, as she lay in bed unable to sleep. I only did it for Joey's sake, at least that's what I've always told myself. But was I being honest? Am I ready to be honest with myself now?

Maybe I should have left here when I

had the chance twenty years ago. But where would I have gone? This is the only place I've ever lived. And Joey was so small, how could I have cared for him alone, without Mom's help? Besides, after the funeral everyone was so comforting, telling me the accident wasn't my fault. 'No one blamed me', they said.

Still, after the story of the 'accident' hit the papers, everything in Ronan changed. The controversy that followed even split the church. A few of the old timers moved away after the accident, and the church split, saying that Ronan wasn't a fit place to live anymore. But most people just went on with their lives, forgetting the accident had ever happened.

Over time, no one spoke of it any more. As if not speaking about it meant it never happened. Eventually I stopped speaking about it. Later I even stopped thinking about it.

I had convinced myself years ago that I was the one to suffer the most from what happened that night, but all along it was Joey who truly suffered. Yes, I lost my husband, but Joey lost his father, and because of the secret this town has shared, he will never know why he has had to suffer.

If I had been honest with myself years ago, then maybe Joey wouldn't have this *need to see Stew as a father figure. Is it too late for me to be honest with Joey now? I don't know. But what I do know is this; good or bad, Stew Thomas is up to something, and I'll just give him enough rope to pull himself up out of the well--or hang himself.*

With that last thought invading her mind, she slowly entered the world of dreams.

CHAPTER SEVEN

A New Star and a New Start

Stew had not slept well. In fact, he had not slept at all. He was afraid to face Marcie, but he had finally faced himself. And he was through running. He was unsure of what the morning would bring, but he was sure he could deal with it, whatever the consequences. Not knowing what else to say, he simply said "Good morning, everyone" as he entered the kitchen. From the expression on everyone's faces, he didn't think that Marcie had exposed his secret. He would have to do that himself. Right after breakfast, he thought.

Marcie did not reveal any hidden emotion as she acknowledged him. "Good morning. We held off breakfast, thinking you'd want to sleep a little extra after last night."

Stew poured himself a cup of coffee

as he looked at the family seated around the table. They had apparently been up for quite some time. "Thanks. I appreciate that, but the ones that need the extra sleep are Buck and Miss Murphy. When it was my second watch with Mr. Sloan, they wouldn't let me. They insisted that he was sleeping comfortably, and they would wake me if there were any problems. They never woke me."

Joey grinned as if he knew a secret that he would never tell. "That's funny; they said the same thing to me."

Marcie was in on the joke. "And me."

Elizabeth was quick to add, "That must be how the tree got decorated. While we slept, they decorated it."

Marcie took a pan of hot cinnamon rolls out of the oven and set them on the table. "Once when I came out to get coffee, I heard them talking and laughing like school children. Apparently, Mr. Sloan's not the only one Doc Stewart's helped lately. I think our good doctor had a plan all along when he put the two of them on the same shift last night."

Stew was embarrassed, but smiled. "Nonsense. It was just practical, is all."

Everyone looked at Elizabeth as she pointed to the living room and exclaimed, "Would you look at that!" Her tone of voice scared her daughter.

"Mom, what is it? What's wrong?"

"Nothing's wrong. Look at the top of the tree."

All eyes turned at once to the fully decorated tree, and the obvious new decoration on the top. Marcie was the first to find her voice, and spoke for everyone. "The star! It's a new star! But how did...?"

Just then, Buck entered with Miss Murphy. For the first time in anyone's memory he had a pleasant expression on his face. His words were harsh, but his voice was soft, or at least softer than anyone had ever heard before. "Oh, quit 'yer jabberin'. It's nothing special. I was just tired of looking at that old star. Thought it was about time it was replaced. The new one was on sale, is all. No big deal."

Marcie added to his embarrassment by gently kissing him on the cheek. She spoke for everyone. "Of course. No big deal. But thank you anyway. It'll be hard to get used to the tree without the old star, though. We've all gotten kinda used to it."

Miss Murphy did not try to hide her excitement as she prodded Buck further. "Oh, it won't go to waste. Buck had an idea."

"Now, Jane." As everyone else looked

at each other and silently mouthed 'Jane' in mock surprise, Buck continued as if he would lose his courage if he stopped. "I don't think this is the time or place to talk about..."

"Sure it is." Miss Murphy was clearly enjoying watching Buck squirm. She turned away from Buck to explain. "Buck figured that since next Christmas he and I are going to have our own tree, we could sort of 'retire' the old star and give it a new life at our place."

The response was a simultaneous "Congratulations!"

Marcie was the first to think logically. "Have you set a date yet?"

"Sometime at the end of the school year. We figured my students may want to be involved."

"I don't see what all the fussin' and carryin' on is about," Buck stammered. "It's just simple logic, is all. We been stayin' here so long together we figured we must be able to tolerate each other."

Marcie clasped her hands around both of theirs. She realized it was the first time she had seen the two of them holding hands. It was a pleasant sight. "I'll miss having the two of you around," she said seriously. She paused slightly before she lowered her voice and continued. "But maybe that's just God's confirmation."

Joey didn't understand. "What do you mean, Mom?"

She waved them all to the seats near the fireplace. "Oh, now's as good a time as any to tell you. Let's be seated. I've got some news for all of you. I was going to wait until after Christmas to say anything, but I may as well tell you now." For just a moment Stew's back stiffened as he realized that Marcie was about to expose his secret. He wondered if he should flee the room, but just as quickly realized that he was too tired of fleeing. He had come to Ronan with a secret plan that he would never fulfill, and it was time for him to admit the fact to himself and to everyone else. And then face the consequences. But Marcie's words were not at all what he expected. Not even close.

Before Marcie could explain, her mother turned to her and said, in a voice that was suddenly old and tired, "Marcie, you're scaring me. Are you ill?"

Stew realized he was holding his breath, and slowly let it out as Marcie answered. "No, Mom. Nothing like that. I'm perfectly fine. It's just that since Jim..." She turned toward Stew. "Jim was my husband. Since Jim died, this hasn't been a working ranch. I've been able to keep most of the land and the outbuildings, but the cattle have been gone for years. The only way I've been able to hold on to the house is to use it as a boarding house. But except for Stew coming to town, no one new has moved here for years. People move away from Ronan, but no one moves to Ronan. Without people moving to town there's just no need for a boarding house. I've decided to sell. I know I can't get what the land's worth, but I can get enough to care for Mom and me somewhere else. Maybe someplace where the winters aren't so bad."

Joey was near tears, and he hated himself for it. Suddenly he didn't feel very grown-up. "But what about me?"

"You're a grown man, son. It's time for you to move on soon. You need to find your own dream."

As Marcie tried to comfort her son, an idea began to grow in Stew's mind. Maybe, just maybe his plan could still work. It would take some readjustment, to be sure, but there was a possibility. He would cling to that. No one in town, not even Marcie, new exactly why he was here. If he could come up with some kind of reason for Marcie not to expose what she knew of him, at least for a little while, it would give him the opportunity to put his revised plan in place. After all, he rationalized, the only part of his secret that she knew was that he was not really Doctor Stewart Thomas. At least, she had not given him any indication that she knew more than that. Of course, Mr. Sloan was still a problem, but he could deal with that when the time came, if necessary.

Stew was brought back to the present by Buck trying to lighten the somber mood. "Say, Joey", Buck was saying, "I, uh, I know it isn't Christmas yet, but I think now may be the time for you to open a Christmas present. It's from all of us, but Doc Stewart picked it out."

Stew realized that Buck was playing right into his new plan without knowing it. Stew chose his words carefully. "It was Buck's idea."

Stew's heart was moved deeply as Buck spoke kindly to Joey, handing him a large box from under the tree. "Maybe it will help you find your own dream."

As Joey opened the box and looked inside, his hands started shaking. "It's a- it's a- I mean, it looks like a..."

Buck laughed at Joey, but Joey didn't mind as he heard Buck refer to him for the second time in a way that he never dreamed he would hear. "We won't know how it looks, Cowboy, until we see it on."

Joey stood a little taller as he put it on. "Thank you, everyone! It's--I mean I..." he could no longer control his conflicting emotions. "I think I need to go check on Mr. Sloan." He handed Buck his hat as he turned and walked down the hallway.

It took Marcie a moment to react, and took her even longer to speak without crying. "I'm sorry, Joey. I just don't know what else that I..." She couldn't finish.

Elizabeth put her arm around her daughter, in part to comfort her, but mostly to stop her from going to Joey. "Leave him alone. He's just had a bad shock. We all have. He'll get over it. This is the only home he's ever had. He'll just have to adjust." Her next words were said as much to herself as they were to Marcie. "We all will."

Stew's words forced Elizabeth and Marcie to face him. "I'm not so sure."

Marcie's confusion registered on her face. "What do you mean?"

It was time for Stew to put his revised plan into motion. If it didn't work, well, the next bus out of Ronan could have him back in New York by early next week. "I have an idea of my own that's been brewing around in my head. I think maybe now's the time to spill it."

Elizabeth's response was short and to

the point. "So spill it."

Stew weighed his words as if his life depended on it. It did. "Coming from New York, I see things a little differently than all of you do. I don't know if this is a good thing or not. Maybe it's just different."

Buck sounded like his old self. "One thing they never taught you in New York is how to talk plain. Will you just start talkin'?"

"Here goes." Stew drew a deep breath and slowly let it out. "You're right, Marcie, people aren't moving to Ronan, but they are going through Ronan when they travel to Missoula or Kalispell."

"So?"

"So take advantage of it." As Stew continued his explanation, he watched from the corner of his eye as Joey reentered the room. Stew kept talking without looking at Joey. Right now, he realized, he needed Marcie to understand every word he said. "Your boarding house is just off the highway. With a little modification, you could turn it into a bed and breakfast. More and more tourists are coming through here, and with Elizabeth's cooking I think you'd have a sure thing."

"That's a wonderful idea, but I..."

"But what?"

With what she knew of Stew, she was not sure she could trust him. She wasn't even sure she wanted to. "Well, even if I can manage to turn this place into a bed and breakfast, that still won't give me enough income. There aren't that many tourists through here."

"I already thought of that. That's where the rest of my idea comes in. Now, Elizabeth, you have a reputation..."

"I have a what!" She had never sounded so shocked.

Stew laughed. "Not that kind of reputation!" Now everyone laughed as Stew continued. "You have a reputation as being the best cook this side of the Rockies."

"Thanks for the compliment, but I don't understand."

"Well, with the tourists going through here, a few of them will want to stop and spend the night, but all of them will want to stop and eat."

"So?"

"So, you're going to feed them."

"Where? This place isn't big enough to..."

"The barn."

"The barn?"

Stew could see clearly that no one was following his train of thought. "Yes. That barn's pretty big. It'll make a nice restaurant. It's too big to be wasted on just Ol' Thunder. I can build him a smaller barn all his own. I know it'll take some work, but I've been learning a lot by renovating that barn in town as my clinic. I figure I can renovate your barn in just a few weeks."

Against her will, Marcie was beginning to share Stew's excitement. Still, with what she knew, how could she ever trust him? "But how? When? Why?"

"I don't know all the answers yet, myself, but I'm working on them."

"Now I don't understand. Why would you want to do this? You don't even really know us."

"But I would like to. Look, it won't be easy and it'll take a lot of work, but..."

Buck jumped in. "Jane and I will help."

"Me too," came from Joey.

Stew was becoming more confident. "I'm counting on it."

Marcie attempted to bring them back to the real world. "Wait a minute. All of you. I appreciate the offer, and maybe it could even work, but the fact is, I can't afford it. At this point I can't even get a bank loan."

Stew answered before Marcie could complete her thought and convince everyone that his idea was not plausible. "I thought of that. I've got the money to…"

"No way! Don't even think that. It's a kind offer, but I'm not going to borrow…"

"Well, apparently it isn't only Montana cowboys that have pride. Just hear me out before you say anything. Then, if you still don't like my plan, I'll honor your wishes."

"All right. I'll listen." They all listened intently as Stew explained his plan to Marcie. Occasionally someone would nod their head in agreement, but no one spoke for fear of breaking the spell.

"I've got some money from my investments in New York. More money than I will ever need. I'll give you…"

"No. Absolutely not."

"…as a loan, whatever it takes for the construction. We can even write out a contract, legal and everything. You can pay me back from the profits as you are able."

"What if there are no profits?"

"Oh, I know there will be profits. Remember, I've tasted Elizabeth's cooking. As for the construction itself, well, that's my Christmas gift to you. As you once said to me, let's work in kind. I'll be your landlord, and you'll be my landlord. What do you say?"

Elizabeth didn't give Marcie a chance to answer. "I don't know what Marcie says, but you've got a deal, Doc."

He had to hear her answer for himself. "Marcie?"

She slowly extended her right hand to reach his hand. As they shook hands, he realized that with her words his plans for Ronan were soon to become a reality. He smiled confidently as she spoke. "Are you about ready to give up your 'Not quite open yet' sign? I think I know someone who can use it." Amid the laughter and shaking of hands, Stew knew that he had won over Marcie. And with Marcie on his side, he knew that he would soon win over the little town of Ronan, whether they liked it or not.

CHAPTER EIGHT

Open For Business

With the help of Buck and Joey, along with Burl and the townspeople he was able to round up, the construction of the clinic was completed a few days later. He had replaced the homemade sign in the window with a new sign that read 'Open for Business'. As Stew worked hanging pictures and doing the necessary 'finishing touches', he thought about how long it had been since he had prayed. Not the quick table-grace kind of prayer, but true heartfelt gut-wrenching God-answering prayer.

Somewhere along the way, he had lost something. He wasn't sure what was missing in his life but whatever it was, he wanted it back. By the world's standards he had always been a good man, at least since he was an adult, anyway. But by God's standards he wasn't so sure. He remembered a small storefront church in New York. How many years ago was that?

His plan for Ronan was now completed. It had worked better than he could have dreamed. While the others had been spending their days working on the completion of the clinic, he had been sneaking off to finalize the arrangements. In the midst of all the activity, no one missed him for the short periods of time he was gone. But now, standing in the lobby of his beautiful new clinic, he did not feel down deep inside where it really counted, as he had expected he would feel. Something wasn't right. Was it because of Marcie that he felt this way? No, he assured himself, that wasn't it. Or maybe it was because of Joey. He felt bad that Joey had begun to depend on him as a son would his father. Stew wondered how Joey would react in a few days, when he revealed who he really was and why he had come to Ronan. But was it his fault that Joey had grown to depend on him? He reminded himself that he had told Marcie he never asked to be Joey's father figure. No, Stew rationalized, he could not let Joey make him feel guilty. At least for something that wasn't his fault. He had enough true guilt to deal with.

No, he told himself, the problem wasn't Marcie or Joey. The problem was Mr. Sloan. He could no longer ignore the situation. Mr. Sloan's health had been improving daily, and it would only be a matter of time, maybe even days, before Mr. Sloan exposed the truth about Doctor Stewart Thomas. Stew knew that he had to convince the town of who he was before Mr. Sloan revealed his own version of the truth. Maybe, he thought, I can go to the newspaper and plead my case. He was still thinking about Mr. Sloan as he started to pray. "Father, God, I don't know what to say except 'Thank You'. I never dreamed I could have the life You have given me. Make my life count, Father. I just want to use all You have given me to serve others. But Father, I don't know what to do about--well, You know what. I just want to forget all about my past, but I know I can't--because I know You can't. At least not until I... Where do I begin? What do I do? I came back here to face my past, and to heal lives where I once hurt them, but I'm afraid. This city has accepted me because they don't know who I am, but if they did, well, only You know what they would do. And Father, about Marcie and what she..."

Joey walked in from the back room carrying a box of supplies. "Doc, where do you want these? This is the last box from the storeroom."

"Anywhere'll be fine. I'll sort through it all later."

"Doc, I know you're the one with the college education and all, but I don't think folks around here are going to be interested in these magazines. Some of these are as old as I am."

"And when was the last time you looked for an updated magazine in a doctor's office?"

"Good point. 'Course, if people want good reading all they have to do is read this morning's town paper. This is the first time I can ever remember anything exciting happening in Ronan."

"What do you mean?"

"You haven't heard? You must be the only person in Ronan that doesn't know. I guess that since you've been spending all your time finishing up here the last few days, you haven't had time to read the papers. We haven't even seen you at home for three days. Everyone's talking about it, Doc. That blizzard back when Mr. Sloan had his stroke."

"What about it?"

"You remember all the roofs on Main Street that caved in from the weight of the snow?"

"So? That's what insurance is for."

"No one around here is able to pay a penny more than necessary for insurance, so there wasn't nearly enough coverage for the cost of rebuilding. Well, someone, anonymously, paid for every bit of the repairs out of his own pocket. No one around here has that kind of money."

"You don't say. I wonder who it could have been? You did say the person gave anonymously."

"Right, anonymously. It couldn't be someone from around here. The reporter did some checking, and could only discover that the money was wired from back East."

Stew thought fast. "Maybe the giver just wanted people to consider it as a gift from God."

"That's what the article said! But how would you know that, unless you...?" As Joey realized the implications of the situation, he understood why Stew did not want to discuss the matter, and felt it best to change the subject. "I have to admit, Doc, you really have learned a lot about renovating. I never thought this old barn could look so good."

"Actually, neither did I."

"Will you be bringing Mr. Sloan here soon?"

Stew hoped Joey could not sense his

stomach muscles tighten. "No need. I'll be sending him home tomorrow. Remember, this isn't a hospital, it's only a clinic. If he stays at the boarding house much longer, your mom's gonna hafta start charging him rent."

"Yah, but I'm beginning to think he likes it there."

"With your Grandma's cooking, what's not to like?"

"True. But it's more than that."

"What do you mean?"

"I don't know, just a feeling I have. I have always thought Mr. Sloan was a mean old man. He may be old, but he's not mean. Not at all. It's strange and I can't really explain it. He just seems comfortable, I guess. Like he enjoys being around people. Maybe he only acted like a hermit because people treated him like a hermit. There may be more to Mr. Sloan than we see."

"I'm sure there is, Joey. Isn't there more to most of us than what we let others see?"

"I guess so. It's strange. I mean, he can't even talk yet, but it's like he's wanting to say something important. His eyes follow me when I enter the room." Joey paused to consider whether to say any more, and then plunged in. "I've noticed something else, too."

"What's that?" Stew asked, not sure he wanted the answer.

"I know it doesn't make sense, since you saved his life and all, but I don't think he likes you. Every time you enter the room, he sorta stiffens up and starts mumbling like a hurt puppy. It's almost like he thinks you're going to hurt him. I know it doesn't make sense. Why would he do that?"

"Maybe I remind him of someone he once knew."

"Maybe." Joey could tell that Stew was uncomfortable, but he couldn't tell why. He looked around the room, as if to give him some clue of something else to talk about. "When do you think you'll be open for business?"

"Soon. I'd like to be open before Christmas, because I want to have your place ready for tourists as soon as possible."

"You can't imagine what your help has meant to my mom and grandma. And me. I've never told anyone this, but, well, uh, I sometimes imagine my father being a lot like you."

"I appreciate that, Joey. You have grown to mean a lot to me. Like the son I never had. I know what it's like to not have a father around when you need him. I'm a grown man, and I still miss my father."

"Is he... is he dead?"

"No, it just seems that way sometimes."

"Then go back to him. Patch things up. At least you still have a chance. I never will."

"It's not that easy."

"Sure it is. Isn't that what you would tell me if I were on the outs with my father?"

"Yes, but..."

"As the saying goes, 'just cowboy up and do it'. I don't know what happened between you and your father, but I know that if I had a chance to have a father, nothing would stop me. Doc, do you know where your father is?"

"Yes, but..."

"No 'buts' about it. Your phone was turned on yesterday. Here, call him."

"I don't know the number."

"That's what 'information' is for. Where does he live? I'll get the number."

"No, I, uh, he can't even, I mean I'd rather pay him a visit. It--it would mean more to him."

"Promise me something, then, and I'll leave you alone about it. Promise me you will see your father before Christmas."

"I promise you that I will see my father before Christmas."

"That's good enough for me."

"Joey, you're as tough to deal with as your mother."

"Where do you think I learned it?"

"Do you know much about your father, Joey?"

"No. Mom doesn't ever talk about him. And she never answers my questions. I think she's ashamed of him, but I don't know why. Grandma just tells me I have to get my answers from Mom. All Mom says is that when I was a baby he did something bad one night--some kind of a stupid prank, I think, with another kid. They were caught. I don't know what happened after that. No one will tell me. I've heard bits and pieces from others. Some say the other kid died or ran away." Suddenly Stew was very sick. He sat down so he would not fall down. It was hard for Stew to concentrate as Joey continued, unaware of what was happening to Stew. "No one has ever told me what happened to my father. It's like the whole town is ashamed of him." Stew was not aware that he had started to fidget with his watchband. Joey was not finished. "All Mom says is that it drew her closer to God after that. She was alone except for Grandma and me, and she learned to depend on God. She's my mom and all, but she's pretty tough. I know her strength comes from God. She'd be the first to tell you that it's been a hard life, but a good one."

Stew put his hand on Joey's shoulder, as much to support himself as to encourage Joey. "Joey, I think I need to tell you something. Something about what happened to..."

The bell above the door rang as Marcie, Elizabeth, and Miss Murphy entered excitedly, carrying packages and a large picnic basket. Elizabeth set down her bundles as she spoke. "We thought you two hard workers might be ready for lunch. We brought a picnic fit for a king-- or at least a cowboy and a doctor."

Stew was anything but hungry. The revelation had hit that his world had just come crashing down on him, leaving no survivors. How could he not have realized who Joey was before now? And that meant that Marcie must be--he shuddered. It couldn't be, but he knew it was. No more questions. No more lies. Everything had to end here and now. Marcie's voice came as a fog in the distance. "This place looks great! You two have really been working. As great as you have this place looking I can't imagine what you'll do to my place. If I had..."

Stew could not let her finish. She must have known the truth--*all* the truth about him, from the beginning. "Marcie, we need to talk. Now! It's important. I need to tell you about..."

How could Miss Murphy interrupt him now? Did she not realize that his life was over? "Whatever it is," she was saying, "it can wait. Your lunch is getting cold. Besides, we have a special Christmas present for you."

Stew knew that there would never be another Christmas for him. Not after today. He could only mumble "It's not Christmas yet."

He didn't know whether Miss Murphy had not heard him or was simply ignoring him. She droned on like a school girl. "We couldn't wait. We all talked about what to get you for Christmas as a thank you for everything you have done for us-- all of us--and we figured this would be the biggest surprise we could give you. Now, close your eyes."

Stew was thinking she was wrong, that it was they who were about to get the biggest surprise, but he forced himself to laugh and go along, for now anyway. "Miss Murphy, I'm not one of your students."

"Hush up, or I'll make you stand in the corner." As Marcie put her hands over Stew's eyes, Miss Murphy continued. "There, ready?"

"Ready." With Marcie's hands over his eyes he could only hear the commotion as the bell above the door once again rang. When will this be over? he thought. There was more commotion as something was dragged or maybe scraped across the floor. He couldn't imagine what was going on, nor did he care. He just wanted this all to end. Now. "I can't imagine what you could all be so excited about. I don't need any..."

"H-h-hello, s-son." Stew sank to a chair amid exclamations of surprise from everyone around him. From somewhere in his fog, he heard Buck, who must have helped Mr. Sloan into the room.

"No, Mr. Sloan, this is Doctor Stewart. He saved your life after your stroke. You remember now, don't you?"

As Buck helped Mr. Sloan to sit, Stew turned to face his judge and jury. He would not plead his case. He knew he was guilty, and it was time for the sentencing. "No, Buck. Mr. Sloan is my father."

Miss Murphy spoke for everyone. "I don't understand."

Joey looked hurt, confused, and angry. "None of us understand. What's going on?"

Stew looked at Marcie, not for understanding, but for an explanation. "I think

Marcie knows. Don't you, Marcie?"

There was compassion in her voice. "At least a little. But this is your story, and you need to tell it. Remember the words from your sermon? 'Speak ye every man the truth to his neighbor.' This whole town has ignored this story for too long. Secret lies must come to the front."

Stew could only repeat a line he had once read. "Ronan is a city of actors. Each man playing his part so well, he no longer remembers he's acting."

Joey was instantly in his face, fierce and raging. "Hey! That's from my journal! You read my journal! I trusted you. I told you I wasn't ready for anyone to read my writing, and you read it anyway. I was wrong about you. I hate you! And I don't want your stupid hat!" As he threw down his hat and turned to storm out of the room, unable to see where he was going through his tears, Stew reached out with his right hand and gently placed it on his shoulder as he picked up Joey's hat with his left hand and placed it back on Joey's head. As Joey turned to face, him he saw that Stew's eyes were also filled with tears, but it was too late for Joey to care.

"Wait, Joey. Let me explain. You may still hate me, but it will be for something I deserve. I didn't read your journal on purpose. I accidentally picked it up when

I thought I was picking up my journal. Remember, they look alike."

When Marcie saw that Joey wasn't listening to Stew, she took charge immediately. "Joey, sit down. We can discuss the journal later. I think there's something more important to discuss here. Go on, Doctor Stewart."

Joey's voice was filled with hate. Or was it pain? Stew wasn't sure. "It doesn't appear that's even your real name. And you called yourself a preacher. I guess that's a lie too! Tell me, *Doctor Stewart Thomas*, is there anything about you that's not a lie?"

Stew had never felt so old. "Yes, Joey, there is. Two things. First, I really am a doctor from New York. Second, I really do care for you, all of you."

"I bet."

Stew's pain matched Joey's, but he forced himself to go on. "I deserve that. I hurt all of you, and I'm sorry for that. I really am."

Joey spat on the floor. "Too late for apologies. I don't believe you. Tell your lies to someone who cares. I'm leaving."

Marcie's voice was firm. "You stay right here, Joey, and hear Doctor Stewart out."

"Why?"

"Because I said so. And because I believe him."

Joey was incredulous. "Why do you believe him? He's lied to us since he came here. You don't even know who he really is."

"Yes, I do." She turned to face Stew and spoke gently, as much to Stew as to Joey. "I know exactly who he is. And I think I know why he's lied to us. And Joey, I've been just as much a part of the lie as he has. Doc knows what really happened to your father. He may be the only man that knows. By my keeping part of the story a secret all these years, I'm just as much to blame as Doc is."

Elizabeth was beginning to understand more of the story. She spoke tenderly. "We all are."

"Grandma, you know about this?"

"Not until just now. I don't have it all figured out, but I'm beginning to put the puzzle together."

Stew just wanted it all to end. "Please, everyone, I need to tell you the whole story." He put his hand on Joey's shoulder and with his eyes he pleaded for Joey to sit. As Joey slowly sank into a chair, Stew turned to face his father. As every emotion within him burst forth he knelt to the floor, placed both hands on the old man's shoulders, hugged him tightly and cried as he had not cried for twenty years. He felt everyone's silence as he took his father's face in his hands. "Father, I'm so sorry. I know I've hurt you most of all. I love you, Dad. I always have."

The old man's voice was strong. His stammer was not from the stroke, but from emotion. "I-I love you too."

As Stew tore himself away from his father to face his jury, he began a story that had been twenty years in the making. "Many years ago, I was maybe fourteen years old, something happened one Christmas Eve. Dad and I had gotten into a fight. I don't even remember any more what it was about. I stormed out of the house and decided to hitch a ride to town. An older teen, I don't even remember his name..."

Marcie revealed softly, "Jim. His name was Jim."

"Jim picked me up and offered me a ride. He had some beer in his truck, and by the time we got to town we were both pretty drunk. He was as angry and upset as I was. He had just had his first real fight with his new wife, and he had stormed out of the house. He told me he had a brand new baby at home, and this would be his first Christmas with his wife and baby. He was real sorry for the fight and he wanted to make it up to his wife, but he didn't know how. It was Christ-mas Eve and he didn't have any money for Christmas presents. We hit on a plan. I don't even remember whose idea it was at the time. Old Man..." he looked at Joey and revised his wording. "Mr. Withers..."

Buck's voice shook as he interrupted Stew. "Withers?"

"Yes. Is that important?"

"Andrew Withers?"

"I don't know. It doesn't matter what his name was. Please, Buck, this is hard enough without you interr..."

"Stew, I have to know. Did he have two sons?"

"Yes, I think so. Why?"

"Stew, I, uh, I..."

"What! Buck, you're making me nerv-ous."

"Stew, I, it's just that, well, remember when you first came here?"

"Yeah. So? What does that have to do with anything?" Stew wasn't sure he wanted to hear Buck's answer.

"Well, I was, I was just concerned about the ladies is all."

"And?"

"And I, I was suspicious of you at first. You were so secretive, remember? Well, when you moved into the house I had to think of the welfare of the ladies. So I, I started asking around about you.

Course, it was just like you said, you having come from New York and all. And no one around here knew anything about you, except..."

"Except?"

"I was at the barber shop just a few days after you moved in to the boarding house, and I was telling the guys there about you. I thought it strange that you had just come to town and you seemed to know a lot about us already. It was when I mentioned that you knew about the fires, both the one in 1912 and the one in 1928 that Ben--Ben Withers--spoke up. Ben is one of Andrew Withers' sons. He wouldn't tell me what he was thinking, but he said he had heard a few things about the new stranger in town and he had his own suspicions to check out. Then he got up and left. He didn't even get his hair cut. Stew, I don't know what story you're about to tell us, but if Ben Withers has anything on you, then you need to hightail it out of town--and I mean now! Ben isn't someone you want to mess with, especially if this has any-thing to do with his dad. I've seen the results of more than one of his drunken brawls. And Ben always comes out the winner."

"Buck, everyone, I'll leave, but not until I've told my story. And, actually, I'm not sure I'll even leave then. I'm through running. I've been running my whole life, even when I didn't know it. Now, I'm going to finish my story and then we can talk about my leaving. But not until then. Understood?"

Buck's mumble was barely audible. "Understood."

Stew took a deep breath before he went on. "Now, Mr. Withers had more sheep than he knew what to do with. We figured he wouldn't miss one little lamb. Jim thought that if he could get a lamb for his baby for Christmas, it would please his wife. We almost got away with it, too. We were feeling the effect of the beer, and it slowed us down. Mr. Withers saw me get caught in the fence with the lamb in my arms. I yelled for Jim to help me. I had never been so scared before. Jim saw that I was stuck and about to get caught by Mr. Withers and his sons. It's important for all of you to know that Jim had not yet been seen by Withers. He could have gotten away, and no one would ever have known he was involved, but he didn't. He chose to come back to help me. Mr. Withers and his sons reached me about the same time Jim did. A fight broke out. Withers had a gun, and somehow Jim was shot."

Joey and Marcie held tightly to each

other, while Buck and Miss Murphy held up Elizabeth.

"Jim gave his life for me. He didn't have to." Suddenly Stew felt very tired.

Joey was the first to speak, barely holding back his anger. "Is that why you came back? To tell me my father was a drunk and a thief? You could have done that and left again, so why stay?"

"I didn't know who you were when I came to town. Even after I met you all, I didn't make the connection. Remember, that day was the only time I had ever met Jim. Joey, I didn't know who you were until a few minutes ago when you told me about your father." Stew looked at Marcie. "But your mom figured it out a long time ago, didn't you?"

Joey refused to believe this. "You knew, Mom? This man killed my father and you let him stay in our home. Why?"

Marcie was aging before their eyes. "Let him finish his story, Joey. I think you'll understand then."

Stew just wanted to finish his story and get back to life, or what was left of it. He suddenly understood how Humpty Dumpty felt. "Back then, there was a tradition in this part of the country. If a man was caught stealing sheep, he was branded." As he continued speaking, he took off his watchband. "Here, Joey, look at this." That's what the ST stands for. Not Stew Thomas or Stallion Trainer. ST stands for sheep thief. I couldn't stand the way people treated me after that night. Especially after Jim's funeral. Joey, remember, I was only a kid. I knew that if I stayed here, I would always be hated and remembered as a sheep thief. People treated Dad differently, too. That was the hardest part of all. Everyone said it was his fault--that he was a bad father. I knew that wasn't true."

Stew kneeled in front of his father and spoke as if he was the only one in the room. "Dad, I couldn't bear what they said about you. I didn't leave because I hated you. I left because I loved you." Stew knew that he was too close to tears and stood to regain his composure. As he spoke, he paced, as a caged animal looking for an escape.

"I thought that if I left, then maybe people would forget about what happened. And I was right, for the most part. When I left, I changed my name from Stewart Sloan to Stewart Thomas, and started over in New York. I wanted a place big enough to hide in. The problem was, the person I was hiding from was still there inside of me, no matter where I went. One night I was wandering the streets and ended up inside a storefront mission, where I was led to the Lord. The mission director was good to me. He helped me go to Bible school and medical school. That never would have happened if I had stayed here in Ronan. Marcie, when we first met I told you about an anonymous benefactor that helped me without even knowing it. That benefactor was your husband. If he had not saved my life that night, I never would have become a doctor. I have spent the last twenty years trying to help people. I even pastored a church for a little while, but my past was always hanging over my head. So I decided that if I was a medical doctor, I could still help people and even have the opportunity to tell them about life with God. That worked for a while. I didn't feel like I had to pretend about my past any more, but no matter how much I tried to get on with my life, I just couldn't get past that night. I had to come back here and try to make things right. I decided that if I came back and proved to everyone that I had changed-- that God had done a work in my life, then I could go on."

Joey looked as if there was a boy inside of him struggling to become a man. He chose his words and his tone carefully. "So even the good things you did here were all a lie. The clinic offering free medical aid, the money to repair the buildings on Main Street, even the work at our place. That was all just part of your act. I guess I was right about the people of Ronan. They are all actors. And you have the starring role."

The pain on Stew's face was transparent. "No, Joey. At least I didn't mean it that way. I sincerely wanted to help people. I never said a word to you about the repairs for the buildings on Main Street. You figured that out on your own. I didn't want to help out at your place to trick you, or get anything from you in return. My offer still stands, if you'll let it. I was just afraid that if everyone here knew who I was right away, then they would never give me the chance to show how God can change a life. Please forgive me. I meant well. I just did it all wrong."

Buck waited for someone else to speak. When no one did, he stepped forward and extended his hand to Stew. "We forgive you," he said, as if for everyone. "I never knew you as Stewart Sloan, so you will always be Doc Stewart to me. I don't care about your past. I know that God has used you to change my life today, and I will always care for you because of that." Stew shook his hand wordlessly.

Miss Murphy offered, "Me too."

"Thank you both" Stew said sincerely.

"But there's still one thing I don't understand."

"What's that?" Marcie asked.

"You. You knew who I was all along, yet you invited me into your home. Why? I'm responsible for your husband's death."

"Stew, you are not responsible for my husband's death. He is. He did not have to come back to help you, but he chose to. Until just now I did not know what happened that night. All I knew was that two drunk kids pulled a stupid stunt that went bad. I will never be glad that night happened, and the memory will always be painful, but God used that event to bring me to Him as my Savior. I knelt at Jim's casket, in the same church you preached in, and gave my life to Jesus Christ. It hasn't been an easy life, but it's been a good life."

Stew took both of her hands in his. There were tears in his eyes, his face wet. "Can you ever forgive me?"

"There's nothing to forgive. I forgave you as Christ forgave me at Jim's casket. I'm just as guilty as the rest of Ronan for playing my part on stage." She turned to Joey and saw him now, not just as her son, but as a man. "I never lied to you Joey, but by not telling the whole story, or at least what I knew of it, I was living a lie also. Joey, please forgive me. I understand why Stew was afraid of us knowing the truth, because I was afraid of you knowing the truth. I thought you would blame me because of the fight I had with your father. The fight that sent him out of the house that night. Joey, I need you to forgive me."

As Joey wrapped his arms around his mother, she heard him whisper, "Like you said, Mom, there is nothing to forgive."

After a long moment, Marcie turned to Stew. "Oh, Stew, I almost forgot. We all chipped in and got you a little Christmas gift."

Joey was his old self again. "Mom picked it out. She was very specific."

"Marcie, everyone, you've already given me the best Christmas gift I could ever receive. How could I take anything else?"

Marcie's twinkle had returned to her eyes. "It's just a little reminder of your new life. But first, there's something I need to do." She slowly and deliberately reached with both her hands to the watch on his left hand wrist. Pulling off his watch and exposing his mark, she put his watch in her left coat pocket. Then she reached into her right coat pocket and pulled out a small package.

As she opened the package, everyone heard from somewhere outside carolers beginning the sweet strains of *Joy to the World*.

As Marcie placed the pocket watch in Stew's hand he just stood there for a moment, mesmerized. His voice was filled with emotion, his face stained with fresh tears, as, turning to everyone, he choked, "It's--it's the most beautiful present I have ever received. But I don't understand."

Marcie and Joey each had an arm on one of his shoulders. Marcie's expression of peace went first to Stew, then to the watch in his hand and finally back to Stew's kind face. "It's time you stopped hiding your past. That isn't who you are any more. God has changed your life."

"But without my watch, when people see my mark they'll see..."

Stew would never forget Joey's next words. "They will see what we see. Doesn't ST stand for saint?"

EPILOGUE

The old man read from the last page of the worn book as Katie rested, nearly asleep, at his feet. He paused as if an almost forgotten memory was once again playing out before him, somewhere beyond the comforts of this room. The voice of the man was old, but once again the emotion of the man was young. So very young. Picking up where he had left off in the story, he blinked away a tear and continued reading. 'And as is true of all good legends, the story has grown with time. But that's not important. What is important to remember is this: one Christmas long ago, a stranger arrived in Ronan, Montana. His love touched everyone he knew. No, he didn't change the world. But he changed his world. He changed Ronan, and he changed me. After awhile, when he knew his time there was finished, he moved on. But that's another story for another time. Everywhere he went, lives were changed.

And the lives he touched, the lives he changed, have continued to touch and change lives all around. But before he left, I was ready to take over the clinic he started. It still isn't much of a clinic, but it's all we need. It keeps me plenty busy. But not so busy that I can't write a book now and then. Maybe you've read one of them. Maybe not. If you're ever passing through this part of the country and you're hungry for a good meal and good company, or just a good story, stop in at the New Heart Inn. It's somewhere about halfway between Missoula and Kalispell. The sign at the city limits still says 'Ronan', but for those of us who live here it will always be known as 'The Healing City'.

The old man slowly closed the book and reached down to pick up Katie, fast asleep, as he heard a familiar voice from the next room. "Joey", she said, "you'd better hurry with that story. Mr. Johnson's son just got thrown again from that horse you gave him. He's bringing the boy into the clinic with a broken arm. I declare, sometimes I think you gave him that horse just so you could stay in business and have a chance to keep sharing the gospel with him."

There was a slight grin on his face as he answered, "Maybe I did, Mom. Maybe I did."

Dr. Joseph Ransom was born in the town of Ronan, Montana, the setting for *The Healing City*, adapted from his stage play of the same name. After graduation from college in Missouri with a degree in Communications, he returned to Ronan to write his autobiography, *I'm Not Really Blind, I Just Can't See*, which has also been adapted as a stage play. He then completed a Master's degree in Religious Education, a Doctorate of Ministries degree in counseling, and a Doctorate of Theology degree. Joseph is the founder of 'Joseph's Closet Ministries' and travels as a Christian dramatist and a motivational and conference speaker. He has authored and produced numerous stage plays.

Currently Joseph resides in Ozark, MO, with his family, where they are in the process of building Serenity View Lodge, a Christian retreat center.

Visit us on the web:
www.josephscloset.com

Other Works from Joseph Ransom

I'm Not Really Blind, I Just Can't See *(Autobiography)*

I'm Not Really Blind, I Just Can't See *(Stage play by Ron Laws, adapted from the novel)*

Building the Church Together *(Seven Weeks of Corporate and Individual Prayer)*

(Stage Plays)

Unto the Least of These *(The story of George Mueller)*

Songs in the Night *(The story of Fanny Crosby)*

Woven in Time *(A Christmas story of love, war, and hope)*

Not Many Noble *(The story of D.L. Moody)*

The Christmas God Came to Dinner *(A true story of war and peace in WW11)*

Trumpets From The Rooftop *(The story of William and Catherine Booth)*

Compelled *(The story of William Carey)*

The Last Oasis *(The story of Lillian Trasher)*

The Healing City *(A Cowboy Christmas Story)*

Toys of War *(The Story of A.C. Gilbert)*

Amazing Grace *(The Story of John Newton and William Wilberforce)*

The Healing City

Printed in the United States
81474LV00001B/28-75

9 781602 640245